Gift of Faith

Gift of Faith

Robert Fleming

www.urbanchristianonline.com

Urban Books, LLC
78 East Industry Court
Deer Park, NY 11729

ISBN 13: 978-1-60162-745-2
ISBN 10: 1-60162-745-9

First Printing January 2013
Printed in the United States of America

10 9 8 7 6 5 4 3 2 1

This is a work of fiction. Any references or similarities to actual events, real people, living or dead, or to real locales are intended to give the novel a sense of reality. Any similarity in other names, characters, places, and incidents is entirely coincidental.

Distributed by Kensington Corp.
Submit Wholesale Orders to:
Kensington Publishing Corp.
C/O Penguin Group (USA) Inc.
Attention: Order Processing
405 Murray Hill Parkway
East Rutherford, NJ 07073-2316
Phone: 1-800-526-0275
Fax: 1-800-227-9604

GIFT OF FAITH

A Novel

By ROBERT FLEMING

The church is like a sturdy tree, only strong as its branches, only strong as its preachers and members.

—Rev. James Bevel (1966)

ACKNOWLEDGMENTS

This book was only possible because of the support and care of Joylynn M. Ross, of Urban Christian. Thank you for the opportunity to write this valuable story of redemption and salvation.

To my mother, Dorothy Woolfolk, my grandmother, Rose Smith, and my great-grandmother, Ida Hollingshead, all women who love the Lord and the church.

To Dr. E. Marie Johnson, the mother of my beloved Donna Johnson.

To my friends and readers, both new and old, who continue to support me and read my books.

And to God, who has protected, guided, and nurtured me in this precious second chance at life. Thank you so much.

In Appreciation of Annetta Gomez-Jefferson,
mentor, a writer supreme, and a friend of the arts

CHAPTER 1

ENDURING THROUGH FAITH

Faith is the substance of things hoped for, the evidence of things not seen.

—Hebrews 11:1

There was nothing wrong with my heart. It was my soul. It was working too hard, coldly avoiding the petty pressures of family life like an idiot, and moving through the adult years with so much speed and no mindfulness. Like so many people, just going through the motions.

After the close of the day, I couldn't wait to get home, the empty home I once shared with my wife and children before "the incident" happened. The incident occurred only a short time ago. My soul was still in pain. I stopped driving my car because of all the medications the doctors had me taking. It was making me woozy, making me forget things. At the insistence of my close friends, I now rode the bus, pushing and shoving to get a seat, jockeying for a window.

Once home, I couldn't tune out the secular world I'd just left, as I placed the solemn words of my plea to the ear of the Divine. I welcomed staying in the moment, being in touch with the small confines of the room and my inner world. I could hear the soft hum of the air conditioner, the traffic outside, and the chirp of young boys tossing a baseball among themselves.

Prayer was therapeutic. It was very healing. Real prayer and its benefit of deep relaxation was the only thing that got me through when the whole world collapsed around me. Those words of comfort and solace and the holy images lifted me up, past the tragedy of my shattered domestic life, away to a place where I could catch my breath and relax.

Sometimes, if I allowed myself to enjoy the magic found in prayer, my mind cleared of all thoughts and pictures. Sometimes, if I permitted myself the luxury to concentrate on the words of the prayer, I found my body coming back hours later from a velvet cocoon of those sacred words, wrapped in a kind of spiritual warmth.

When my eyes read the words of comfort found in the scripture of Hebrews 13:5, I felt less alone, less isolated:

Be content with such things as you have. For He Himself has said, "I will never forsake you."

For a while, I felt like I was back in control again, even if I was not.

As my minister told me, isolation and loneliness are some of the worst of human emotions. They gnaw away at your soul, your heart. He was right. During these painful events, our faith must stand like a solid brick wall. In those times, I thought God had left my side, totally abandoned me. Even if the world snatched away my loved ones, my pastor reminded me that I was never alone. Still, I kept hearing the small, wee voice that He was gone from my life. Forsaken me?

One evening only nine months ago, Teresa, my wife, was waiting for me in the parking lot at the church. She was beautiful as usual. Her attire was always smart and current. Not trendy. It was her pinched facial features that let me know that something was wrong. There were bags under her eyes, worry lines along her lovely mouth, and she spoke a mile a minute.

She reached over to her purse and got a cigarette. "We need to talk."

"When did you start smoking again?" I asked. She stopped her addiction for cancer sticks years ago.

"My horoscope says the next move I make might be the most important I make in years," she chattered, watching the traffic stop at a light. "It also says that I should take my time and think before I act."

"When did you start smoking again?" I repeated. "You know it's no good for you, especially with your asthma. You always get bronchitis from it. Always."

She ignored me. "And the horoscope says that if I make the wrong move, then I would regret it. I bet you don't know what sign I am."

"I don't know. Taurus or Scorpio or Leo. Leo, right?" I walked over to the car and got in. She followed me with a scowl on her face.

"Right, it's Leo," she snapped. "Clint, you ignore me. You're more involved with the kids, work, your boss, and your parasite friends. You totally ignore me. I'm on the back burner."

"Where did you get that from?" I asked. The car filled with choking cigarette smoke and I sneezed.

"It's true. I see it every day." She blew two rings into my face.

"Is this what your shrink is telling you?"

She looked straight ahead and frowned. "She says you are completely indifferent to me, that you no longer care. When was the last time you kissed me when you left for the day? You don't give a darn about me."

I scratched my head, giving her a bewildering look. *Where are you getting this stuff from? Who is filling your head with this garbage?*

"We live in the same house but we don't do anything together," she remarked angrily. "It's like we are two college roommates who are polite to each other, raise the kids, but rarely cross one another's paths. We never have any quiet time, romantic time, for ourselves."

I shrugged. "You know, our schedules keep us busy."

"Maybe you could reduce the number of extracurricular activities on your plate and find some quality time for me," she said. "Say no to some of these people who want your time. Streamline your life. Find time for me."

"You never said anything before," I said weakly.

"I just want you to cut back on some activities and spend some time with me," she demanded. "Is that asking too much? You spend entirely too much time at the church. Why? I don't understand it."

"I'm a Christian and all that goes with it," I said proudly.

"It's all about the church and work," she sneered. "Where do I fit in?"

I repeated my earlier protest. "You never said anything before."

"Because we don't talk. When I do talk, you look at me like I have two heads and both of them are stupid. You act like I'm speaking a foreign language. Or you find something else to do while I'm talking. You're always distracted by something. You never listen."

"Yes, I do listen. I pride myself on being a good listener." I was ticked off that she would accuse me of being an inconsiderate husband.

She sulked. "You might listen to other people, but not to me. I want this marriage to work. I don't want to have another woman raising my children or to remarry another man. I want you and that is driving me crazy."

"But what does the church have to do with every-thing?"

She opened the car window and tossed the cigarette out and lit another one. "I spent much of my teens in mental wards or foster care. All I remember is taking pills, stimulants, antidepressants, antipsychotics, and mood stabilizers. I had a tortured, gloomy life. When I met you, I figured the sun would shine on me for once. Wrong. Very wrong."

"I cannot be your rescuer, only the Lord can do that."

"You don't understand what I'm saying," my wife said, her eyes darting from the burning cigarette to my face. "My life is falling apart. I feel like I'm dissolving right before my eyes. I'm tired of crying."

I looked at her in detail, possibly for the first time since sitting in the car. She had the look of a frightened fawn. "Is your shrink helping at all?"

She lowered her eyelids and spoke in a dull mono-tone. "She cannot help me. Nobody can. Only you can. Do you remember when all of the meds were having the side effects? And the docs said they had to pursue another course of treatment. When I went off the medi-cation, the depression came back and I almost killed myself. I was hospitalized three times."

"I remember, Terry," I said. I recalled she had a series of electroconvulsive therapy treatment. Shock treatment. She was never the same after that. Her fa-ther insisted she undergo it. She never disobeyed her father.

I looked at her closely, very closely. She knew how to dress well, but I could tell she was skin and bones underneath. Very, very thin. *When did she stop eating? How long has this depression been worsening?* She was very emotional, always on the verge of tears.

"I'm glad you're my husband, lover, and friend, but I have to leave you," my wife insisted. "It is the only way."

"The only way to do what?" I didn't know what she was talking about. Her thinking was all confused.

"To keep our love alive. . . ." Then she started crying and would not stop. No amount of kind words, gentle embraces, or tender caresses could soothe her pain inside.

Three weeks later, Terry, my wife, strangled our two young children, our three-year-old daughter, Selma, and our five-year-old son, Omar, in our bedroom. She then set fire to the kitchen and living room before stabbing herself repeatedly and slashing her throat. The police found her sprawled on the living room couch, with a hunk of electrical cord in her hands. And the bloody butcher knife nearby.

The cops said my wife did the slaughter but they were hard-pressed to come up with a motive. Neighbors in the building were shocked to learn about the crime. One guy from the third floor said he thought somebody else did it, that a good mother could never have killed her children in such a way.

It had been nine months since that dark day. I was amazed at how rapidly the days of our existence passed. Still, the tragedy had refused to release its grip on my soul. The wound deep inside still ached and sent pain throughout my limbs, organs, and mind.

Aunt Spivey once told me that the present is the moment we are enjoying and nothing past that point is promised. Live fully, live deeply. Learn from the bitter and sweet lessons life offered. I prayed and prayed, using my beloved aunt's adage as a balm for my agonized soul. Live fully.

Then the phone rang. The world intervened on my solace.

A sleepy feminine voice spoke over the receiver, her molasses tone blending with the hiss of the telephone static. "Mr. Clint Winwood, I'm calling on behalf of your aunt. She requests that you pay her a visit. She says she has something important to tell you."

"What day?" I asked her.

"Tomorrow," the senior center official said. That was not a request but an order. A royal command.

After I hung up the phone, I returned to my prayers.

During the words of my prayer, I noted another surge of warmth come over my body, starting with my feet and up to my legs. I had reached this state of awareness before, shortly after Terry's suicide. Quite calm. It was as if I had taken flight, above the clouds, looking down on the roofs. The time spent in traditional bereavement counseling led me down to a series of truths about myself, my selfish ways, my dead ends of wacky reason, all because I couldn't shake the emotional pain of grief and trauma.

In the months following the funeral of my family, I couldn't eat or sleep or function at my job. My boss gave me a lot of leeway, allowing me to take off without the proper protocol. I couldn't focus or concentrate on anything. I developed a severe ache in my chest that didn't permit me to breathe freely.

"You need to embrace the Lord," advised Aunt Spivey. "Grieving has made you off balance. Everything gets to you. You're mentally overwhelmed. You no longer see the world as it is. Only the Lord and earnest prayer can make you whole again. Finding Him will strengthen you and put you on the road to healing."

Terry never prayed. She didn't trust God or organized religion. She had no need for a minister or pastor, but enlisted a group of healers. A Thai practitioner

of Eastern medicine. An acupuncturist from Latvia. A
British homeopath with ties from Johns Hopkins. And
three Colombian shaman who specialized in the cur-
ing of the auras and the human energy field. A former
Taliban princess who specialized in hugs of an ethereal
nature. Hugs that could cure.

That mind-body connection failed to save the lives of
Terry and our children. I looked on and did nothing. I
thought Terry would find the means to save herself. I
never considered she would go down in flames.

The talk from my family turned poisonous as far as
Terry was concerned. I hated to be around my kinfolks.
With bitterness, Aunt Spivey said Terry willingly wel-
comed the Antichrist into our lives and it cost our fam-
ily big time. She added that I must understand that the
Lord was always on our side.

"The Lord cries with us when we are in pain," my
aunt said. "Remember that. Never feel that the Lord is
punishing you. Never think of what has happened to
you as something that you brought on yourself."

Prayer made me understand my pain. When I went
through Terry's things, I sought to understand why she
had done what she did. Maybe I would find something
that would solve the riddle of her actions. I searched
through her suitcases, purses, hatboxes, jewelry cases,
even her treasured package of her scented letters and
notes at the rear of her closet.

There I found this list, scribbled in her swirling scrawl:

MY SERENITY LIST
1. Nothing but the truth
2. The whole bag of tricks
3. Out of fear and guilt
4. The easy way out

5. Never forget
6. In the event of disappointment
7. Sustained applause
8. The life we'd done together
9. Any of the whys and wherefores
10. Not petty or a gossip
11. To exceed one's self
12. The pleasure he has given me

I flipped the list—done on a yellow sheet of a legal pad—over and over. My eyes and mind still didn't comprehend any of the phrases on it. The list never calmed the inner struggle going on in her: the depression, anxiety, panic attacks, agitation, aggressive moodiness, dangerous impulses, rapid-fire talking, abnormal thoughts, hallucinations, confusion, or the feeling about suicide.

Grabbing a box of matches, I held the list and walked to the bathroom. I placed the sheet of paper into the sink, looked at the words as the match flame charred them into an ash. Looking up at the window, I noticed the snowfall was coming much heavier, covering the branches of the barren trees with a brilliant whiteness.

The list was burned. I cursed her to hell. *Why would she do something like this? Damn her soul.* I sat on the edge of the tub with the deepening quiet echoing in my place, and thought about my visit to my beloved aunt. Slowly, the sadness rose up in me, and I covered my face and cried without stopping.

CHAPTER 2

AN AUNT'S PROPHESY

If we confess our sins, He is faithful and just to forgive us our sins and to cleanse us from all unrighteousness.

—1 John 1:9

The January snow was really coming down that next day. Along the highways, my car crept around the automobiles stuck in drifts, between two large trailers overturned, and a major collusion between a Jeep and a cargo truck. The side roads were totally impassable. I was careful to keep my windshield wipers uncluttered from the sludge so I could see the vehicles ice skating wildly across the road.

It took me almost three hours to get from the city to Aunt Spivey's senior center in the highlands upstate. Westchester County. Tired, I pulled into the parking lot, which had not been plowed yet, with cars and vans jammed into a jagged line amid the piles of caked snow. The air was frigid.

I walked quickly across the lot, hatless, moving toward the large Art-Deco building, which was formerly a residence for a grade-B actor who fled east from Tinseltown. The entrance was one of those electric sensor jobs: when your foot would break the laser, you could come forward to the security desk. A couple of stout men, appropriately suited, stood nearby.

"Mrs. Spivey, please," I said. "Could you tell me where she is?"

"In her room, at her quiet hour," the receptionist replied.

"What is the procedure? Can I go up? Can she be disturbed? Or would you rather I wait? Which?"

The woman glanced at one of the guards and then turned to me, saying, "Wait." She was very proud of her crisp white uniform and her rank among the nurses. She didn't have to deal with any of the residents, just the stupid public.

A rotund man, with horn-rimmed glasses and tufts of blond hair over his ears, walked up to me, with a notebook under his arm. "I guess you're the nephew, Clint. Your aunt can be a real handful. Depending on her mood, she can be really difficult, but if you catch her on one of her good days, she can be an angel."

We walked to the elevator and blended into the crowd there. The doctor was talking about her case, her quirks, her flaws, her medical ailments, and her advancing years. No one knew how old she was. She was born in the Deep South at a time when they didn't keep official records.

"How old do you think she is?" the doctor asked me.

"I really don't know." I shrugged.

"Are you the only family she has?" the doctor asked. "You're the only person who has visited her in over eight years."

"I would have visited her sooner but I didn't know where she was," I said. "We still have some family. Some of her old sorority buddies said she has gone back down South. Possibly Atlanta or Charleston."

We got off on the fourth floor. You could hear a pin drop. The quiet was deafening. I imagined that the rooms of the residents were soundproof, insulated to muffle any shouts or screams, so a nurse or attendant couldn't hear them. I surmised that the interior of the living spaces were televised so their activities could be monitored.

"It's so quiet," I said.

"Believe me, we know what's going on at all times." The doctor chuckled. "We have our ways. Nothing misses our attention."

"I see," I replied and let myself be led to a reinforced glass window in a series of similar portholes.

We watched the old, wrinkled black woman through the window. She sat in a wheelchair, motionless, with a vintage copy of *Ebony* magazine across her lap. Eartha Kitt was on the cover, riding a bike. Her well-toned legs were the first thing I noticed about the photo.

I noticed that my aunt wore clean white gloves, the kind that the old ladies wore at church. She was dressed in the drab yellow uniform of the senior center, for the house rule mandated that the residents couldn't wear their own clothes.

The doctor opened the door to her room and announced her visitor. I walked over to my aunt with a bounce in my step and kissed her on her withered cheek. She smiled and stared at me warmly.

"They say I'm difficult so I didn't think they would let me get visitors." She grinned. She said that remark for the benefit of the doctor, who scurried away.

"I came as soon as I got your call." I pulled up a chair. The room was sterile, antiseptic, and almost bare. I couldn't see how someone could call this room home.

"I've been thinking a lot about you, Clint," my aunt said. "Your blood flows in my veins and vice versa. We've got a lot of history in our bloodline. Did you know my mother was one of the ten thousand colored folks who marched down Fifth Avenue to protest the lynching of Negroes? Did you know she was a member of the NAACP before it became a big organization?"

"No, I didn't," I answered. "When was this?"

"About 1917," she continued, turning her wheelchair to face me. "Or my father organized the Brotherhood of Sleeping Car Porters with A. Philip Randolph? He was very good friends with W.E.B. Du Bois and Paul Robeson."

"I'm sure that you didn't bring me out here to discuss family history," I said. "That's not like you. I know you always get straight to the point."

She folded up the magazine, handed it to me, and motioned for me to place it on the nightstand. Her stare was penetrating. "Have you been saved?"

"Sure I have," I answered. I was acting in the capacity of junior minister at my local church, a position that I had held for three years.

"Do you accept the Lord as your personal Savior?"

"Yes," I said, smiling.

"Do you believe the Bible is the Word of God?" my aunt asked.

"Oh yes."

The old woman kept me on my toes. "I've been thinking about you so much because everybody tells me how you have been suffering after this horrible thing your wife did to you. I have my spies. They say you are just going through the motions with your life. It's almost as if you have been crushed by the weight of your guilt and suffering."

I looked down at the gray tiles on the floor. "I'm getting by."

"The heck you are," she bellowed. "You're acting like a sad sack."

"I don't think I am." I glanced up at her.

"All of this pain and suffering . . . self-pity, black moods, hurt feelings, resentment, remorse, guilt, feeling noble because it hurts so good. Clint, you've got a martyr complex. Look at yourself. I'll tell you: nothing changes in this world through pain and suffering."

My eyes returned to the floor. "I just want to numb myself out. Can you understand that?"

"Yes, I can," she said. "You think you've ruined your life. But you're wrong. Your life is just beginning."

"Right," I said it as if she was dead wrong. Telling a boldface lie.

"Yes, I am right." She grinned at me.

"I need to heal," I admitted. "I need to get my head on straight. I'm hurting inside and nothing seems to ease that pain."

"Clint, I don't think you really knew the woman you married," my aunt said. "Terry was a tigress. She was selfish, reckless, and more than slightly crazy. I don't think you understood this. She never knew if you hurt another person, you hurt yourself. As a wife and a mother, she refused to see if she hurt herself, she hurt everybody around her."

Sometimes I feared my wife, maybe because I didn't understand or couldn't control her. I knew Dr. Smart's warning that evil had somehow taken hold of Terry. She had lost her sense of right and wrong. Even the elders pointed out that I needed to recognize and call evil for what it was.

"I knew she had problems," I said. I remembered Terry sitting before the mirror, madness in her red-rimmed eyes, smearing tons of pancake makeup and lipstick all over her face. I saw four half-emptied cups of black coffee and a saucer of prescription pills at her elbow. If I could have recognized her loose grip on her sanity, I would have gotten her help.

She was still stunningly beautiful, even while she was off balance. I thought she was barely holding on. Something was wrong with her.

"Do you think Terry was evil?" I asked her.

"Probably she was," she replied. "We don't come into life knowing how to lie, cheat, or steal. We have free will, the ability to choose both good and evil. When you choose evil, you reject the ultimate choice of accepting the love of God. You see, God allows evil in the world because He loves us."

"That's plenty to wrap a person's head around," I admitted. "All I know is that this is a world in turmoil and it seems that all the forces of evil are free and powerful. I know that."

"Why do you feel so guilty?" My aunt was now searching my eyes with her own stare. I was thinking of how much I failed my wife.

"I could have done something," I mumbled. "I know I could have done something to save her. And my kids." The only thing in my mind was a faded image of Terry sitting at the kitchen table talking gibberish to a salt shaker.

My aunt frowned. "Your wife, Terry, was at war with God. She wanted everything her own way. She wanted to do what made her feel good. She would do anything to give her pleasure. She was selfish."

She watched me whip myself inside. After this tragedy, I was knocked down, leveled, and cursed the day I was born. I was lost. I wanted to wallow in my misery and live my life with God.

"So you going to feel sorry for yourself for the rest of your days," she said harshly. "In this life, things are never certain or permanent. Nothing lasts. And you never know what will happen. Everything changes."

"I know that." I was getting irritated.

She folded her hands and sighed deeply. "Your father was in and out of your life as you were growing up. I remember you as a very skinny kid with that military haircut that your granddaddy used to give you. But always neat and clean. Probably you have good memories of him."

"He was a good man," I recalled. But I always remembered he was a stern disciplinarian, froze you with a sharp rebuke or a snap of his fingers.

"I guess you get your spirituality from him," she said. "He was gruff on the outside but very compassionate and fair on the inside. His word was his bond. When he started having his strokes, I didn't think he was going to last enough to see you get married but he was there."

"He was dead on one side and had to use a cane," I said. "Yes, he was there. He warned me to not to marry Terry. Said she would be nothing but trouble. I didn't listen to him."

"Terry was one hot number." She laughed. "When you're a young buck, the flesh part of a woman is all that matters. And she had curves in all the right places. You were a goner before you gave her the engagement ring."

"I know it." I grinned. "But why did you summon me here?"

"I know I wanted to talk to you about your father," she said. "Do you know anything about him and what his life was like before he fathered you?'

"No, not really."

"Well, let me fill you in on him," she said. "He was a minister like his father before him. He used to tour the country, speaking to church groups, civic organizations, students, and halfway houses. He specialized in talking to juvenile girls who had fallen on bad times.

Anyway, he was busted for writing bad checks. There was a picture of him being led from a plane in handcuffs."

"My grandfather showed me that," I said. "He also showed me the newspaper clippings where Dad said it was a misunderstanding with an old business associate. My father said he knew he carried baggage from his former life but he triumphed over those earlier transgressions to forge a new career."

"Do you know what your father did before he found the Lord?" she asked me. "He was a heartless con man."

"My grandfather said my father wasn't a bad man," I protested. "He also said my father didn't do anything wrong. My father thought it was going to blow over, this trouble, so he could resume his work for the Lord."

"But it didn't," she said. "In the end, it made him a nobody. He didn't want to fight for his reputation."

"Why?" I knew my father had disappeared for a long time after that.

She didn't reply. It was like she didn't want to know everything at once. Families have their secrets.

I nodded, with a concerned look on my face. "So why did you summon me here?"

She moved her wheelchair closer to me, so that she could touch my hand. "I've lived my entire life in the church. I did missionary work in Africa, Nigeria, Kenya, Ghana, Congo, and the Ivory Coast. Even did some work in the Philippines, Japan, and Indonesia. I've lived my life for the Lord. There is a lot of suffering out there."

"I know." I beamed. "I'm proud of you. I've always been."

She patted my hand and looked again in my eyes. "You've got to put aside your suffering and reach out to those who have turned their eyes from God. Those lost souls. They are not living by the Golden Rule. Then there are those baptized men and women who are fooling themselves that they are saved because they are church members. They are worse than the sinners. They cut up on Saturday night and sit in church on Sunday just as big as you please."

"Aunt Spivey, what does that have to do with me?"

She grinned. "The Bible says, 'The Lord will fight for you; you need only to be still. Be still and hear the voice of God. He's a very patient God.'"

"I pray, pray, pray, but I get no answer," I muttered. "Nothing at all."

She shook her gray head. "Remember God knows your future and all your tomorrows. If you yield to His control and trust in his plans for your future, you will be all right. Don't be afraid. If you let go and let God, you need not worry. Stop worrying."

"I'm worn out." I sighed.

"You're young still and you can make a difference," she said. "You've got a good mind, a willing heart, and a sense of purpose. You care deeply about other people. Otherwise you wouldn't let this horrible thing affect your life like it did. I've been on the phone with your senior pastor, Reverend Smart, and he agrees with me that you should be doing your Father's business."

"When did you talk to him?" I was upset at this intrusion.

"Last week, he agreed with me that you should be glorifying His name and spreading His Word. We know there is work to be done, especially among our people. We have lost our souls. We have no memory of our history, our tradition, our community, or our church. We have no love for ourselves or our young. Or our old. We have embraced Satan."

"I agree with you, but I don't think I'm the man for the job," I confessed. "My faith is a bit shaky right now."

"The Reverend Dr. Smart says he will help you find yourself and provide you with everything you need," the old woman added. "Clint, you could be one of His prophets, helping to bring peace and serenity to our people. You could prepare them for the last battle. You could properly prepare them for Armageddon because you've known pain and suffering."

"That I have," I admitted. "It's true that we've come to doubt our humanity but I don't know what I can do about it."

"All I ask you is to look truthfully at yourself, just put aside your guilt," she pleaded. "You could be an effective messenger for a just and living God."

"That's not true. I'm a sinner."

She waved me off, discarding my reasoning. "God can permit suffering, pain, and evil. It's all a test. We're all sinners. We're all wrapped in the original sin. But the grace of God can save you and others through you."

"I let her die and the kids too," I moaned.

"You have to forgive yourself," she said. "You have to forgive her if you're going to survive. This hurt is tearing you up inside. Once you deal with your pain, you can deal with the pain of others. That pain is a bad habit that will keep you stupid and confused. Let it go."

"But I can't," I grumbled. "Nothing I can do will bring them back. I miss Terry and the kids. I truly miss them."

My aunt patted me on the hand again, trying to console me when there was a knock at the door. Two elderly women entered the room, with one carrying a chunk of cherry cobbler wrapped in Saran Wrap. They were bright and bubbly and full of chatter.

"Is this Clint you been talking about?" the woman with the pie asked. "The nurse said you had company and we had to come up and see."

My aunt nodded and smiled.

"Brought you some pie," the other one said to me. "You can nibble on it on your way back to the city. It's tasty."

"Thank you, ladies." I smiled, feeling grateful.

"Now, he's the man who lost his wife and children not long ago," the woman with the pie said. "I think his wife was a crazy tramp who killed the kids. Right?"

My aunt flashed the woman a glaring mean look that said to shut up.

"And then she killed herself," the other one chimed in. "She was a coward who couldn't face the music."

My aunt ignored the women and gave me an affectionate expression to let me know that she had meant me no harm. "Clint came to visit me and I can't tell you how much this has meant to me. We don't have much family left. Did I tell you that he is a minister?"

"He has a church?" the women asked.

"Not yet," my aunt answered. "But he will have one soon."

"Praise be, a man of the Lord," the woman said, handing me the plate with the pie. "Colored folks need deliverance and salvation."

I let my breath out slowly. This visit had been much more than I thought it would be. However, I was totally unprepared for the family revelations, the urgent pleas for my renewed commitment to my faith, and the insults against my troubled late wife. I stood up and stretched.

"Ladies, thank you for the pie," I said, smiling broadly.

The women giggled and told me to enjoy the pastry.

Then I hugged my aunt around her shoulders, whispered that I loved her, and that I would stay in touch. We exchanged grins. A profound sadness went through me when I thought about having to drive back to the city over the icy roads. That would be a real task.

My aunt looked at me with sorrow in her eyes. When her visitors departed her room, she covered her wrinkled face, groaned, and went off to the kitchen to put water on for her mint tea. Maybe it was time for one of her stories, one of her favorite soaps, *General Hospital*.

CHAPTER 3

OPPOSITES ATTRACT

Now abide faith, hope, love, these three; but the greatest of these is love.
—1 Corinthians 13:13

Terry. Terry. Terry.
Where did we go wrong? What happened to us? What happened to her? The contrast between the young girl, just barely legal, standing there in her family's home, and the mature woman, my wife, living in the world was very apparent. The young Terry was alive, vibrant, and full of energy. Under the rigid control of her parents, she became quiet, soft-spoken, quite demure.

When I first met Terry, she was very young. Slightly over twenty. I knew better than to pursue her then, so I watched others chase after her to no avail. Physically, she was stunning, easy on the eyes, with a wildness and confidence just waiting to come out. On the eve of her twenty-first birthday, I ran into her at a free Central Park concert of traditional gospel music sung by local choirs, singing the hymns made famous by such icons as Mahalia Jackson, Dorothy Love Coates, Ernestine Washington, Clara Ward, Sallie Martin, The Swan Silvertones, Albertina Walker, and the Dixie Hummingbirds. She was with a date, probably handpicked by her father. The young man, dressed in a business suit, seemed out of place in the crowd. Everyone was having a good time. He tried to restrain her as she yelled and waved in my direction.

I was alone as usual. However, I didn't go over to her; instead I waited for them to pass as they left the park. We talked quietly and made a date to see each other later. That Saturday afternoon couldn't come quick enough. We sipped coffee and ate frosted crullers and tried to do a shorthand analysis of each other's lives.

"How old are you, Mr. Man?" she asked.

"I'll tell you my age if you tell me yours," I answered. Although I knew she was of legal age, I decided to go slow.

"You know my age," she said. "It's not fair. I thought we were going to be honest with each other. No fibs. Nothing false. I don't want to think you're like these other idiots who only want to get into my panties."

"I'm not like that," I protested.

And I truly believed that. Most of the young men I knew didn't want to get married. They wanted to hook up, wanted friends with benefits, a simple hookup and score with no thought of a long-term relationship. I wanted something more. I wanted something more committed, wanted something that would lead to marriage and family. I needed that intimacy that would lead to the sanctity of the altar and vows.

"Remember that fella you saw me with at the gospel concert in the park?" she said drily. "All he wanted was to score, spend the night together, and go our separate ways. When I told him no, he almost got violent."

"I'm not like that," I repeated.

She smiled shyly and wondered aloud, "I bet my father would like you, and he doesn't like a lot of people, especially the guys I bring home. I hope you don't have too many skeletons in your past. That'll freak him out."

After several weeks of sporadic dates, I was finally invited to her house, out in the frontiers of outer Queens, a gorgeous roomy Colonial structure with a spacious living room with glistening hardwood floors, four bedrooms, and a full, furnished basement. It had a large rear deck suitable for a barbeque party and covered front porch. I was impressed that the place had a garage that could house three cars. A crew of three kept the landscape pristine around the house.

"Oh man, what a house," I exclaimed. "Your father must be very rich. This puts where I come from to shame. I'm from humble, modest beginnings."

"This is nothing," she said with a sense of pride.

Her old man was a big-shot lawyer, raking it in from slum landlords, crooked business types, and well-heeled gangsters with drug money. He showed me into his den after the introductions were made, gave me the once-over, and then proceeded to make himself a martini. I noticed he didn't offer me one, not that I would have taken it.

"To be a real black man, you must be a warrior," her father started in his deep-bass summation voice. "You must be a breadwinner. I take care of my family. I want to know that my little girl will be well provided for. I take that very seriously."

I sat there on the sofa very stiffly. "Yes, I do too."

"Dream big," he continued. "Make your own way in the world. Forget about the craziness of rage and anger against the white man. That will do you no good."

I nodded passively, saying nothing.

"Don't clam up." He took a sip from his drink.

I cleared my throat, suddenly losing the power to speak.

"Do you want my girl?"

I replied weakly, "Yes, sir."

"What are your intentions toward her?" He stared directly into my eyes. I was forced to stare back at him in order to prove that I was worthy. I didn't want to come across like a wimp.

"Very honorable, sir," I replied.

"Can you treat her right, decently, honorably, in the manner that she is accustomed to?" The stare was unceasing, intense.

"Yes, I will, sir."

He speared the olive and bit into it. "What does your father do for a living?"

I swallowed hard. "He's a pastor, among other things."

Her father frowned, suddenly lost in thought. His voice was quiet and challenging, with an edge to it. "It's not enough to get by. We as men must win. We as a proud race must succeed."

I smiled, a nervous habit of youth. "Not everybody wins."

"Some of our people don't have the stuff to win," he said, almost angrily. "Some of us are natural losers. They don't deserve to win or succeed."

"I guess," I replied. I hated this kind of class-conscious stiff who had written off half of our people to suit themselves. Only they could make it in the white man's world.

"Do you think the world owes you something?" her father asked, serious. "Are you one of those black boys who think Mr. Charlie is going to give you something?"

I hated this interrogation. "No. I believe in work. I believe you must earn your success. I'm a hard worker."

"So what are you going to do with your life?" His glare was full strength on me now.

Suddenly, I felt a knot of nausea, bitter and foul in my mouth, but I refused to give in to it. I wasn't used to having someone press me like this. Like a mean-spirited cop trying to break down a young black kid to confess to a crime.

"I want to spread the Word of God," I solemnly confessed.

Blinking wildly, her father stood up, facing me, and lit a cigarette. "I don't think you're good enough for my daughter. She's fragile. She has big dreams and hopes. She deserves much better than you."

"Why don't you give me a chance?" I pleaded.

"For what?"

"To prove myself," I replied. "I'm young. I want to prove to you and your family that I'm worthy of your daughter."

"Why should I give you anything?" He sneered at me like a bug about to be smashed.

"Because you're a fair man," I answered.

"Bull." He laughed rudely. "I'm not fair and life surely is not. You're setting yourself up to fail. You're a loser."

"No, sir." I wanted to punch him. I fought the urge to slug him and knock him on his butt.

His face was a mask, solid and impenetrable. "I cannot take chances with my little girl. Not with her life. Not with the likes of you."

"What am I supposed to do?" I asked him. I loved her.

"Find another girl, thug," he said sarcastically. "Leave my daughter alone. You're no good for her."

"Pardon . . ." Defiantly, I stared at him, stood, and walked out. I never went back to that house. The dinner we were supposed to eat was cancelled. Her father never even asked me my name.

In two months, we were married in a civil ceremony at City Hall, but later tied the knot at the summer house of Dr. Smart on Long Island. Some of my family attended the second event, but none of Terry's clan could make it. For three days and nights, my bride cried herself to sleep, refusing to leave the bed.

CHAPTER 4

WELCOME TO OUR TRUTH

Let him ask in faith, with no doubting, for he who doubts is like a wave of the sea driven and tossed by the wind.

—James 1:6

Looking at the children playing on the lawn, Terry narrowed her eyes and said quietly, "When you're eighteen years old, you think you know it all, but then when you get older, you realize you don't know a thing. You're as a stupid as those kids out there."

This was only four months before the tragedy. A lot had changed. She was now sad, distracted, and very thin. Her eyes had dark circles around them. She rarely ate and when she did, it was Almond Joy candy bars. After we would go to bed, I would find her sitting in the bathroom, whispering into the cell phone to someone.

"Who are you talking to, sweetie?" I asked her, stifling a yawn.

"None of your business," she snapped.

"I think I have the right to know," I insisted.

"No, you need to mind your own business," she said while holding a hand over the phone so whoever was on the other line would not hear.

This was not the idea of marriage that I signed up for, two distinct people pulling in opposite directions.

I knew Terry was a spoiled brat when I took her away from her home and family. I knew she was extremely self-centered. It didn't matter how much we talked because she had her notions of the picture-perfect life she wanted to live and nothing was going to mess that up for her.

I told my aunt that I thought she took the blessing of a loving, caring family for granted. Maybe I was being too responsible. All I wanted was to iron out our disagreements and obstacles and move to a common ground. Compromise. Terry hated that word. It meant weakness and softness.

"Turning the other cheek, right?" she taunted.

In the beginning, Terry was perfection. She was everything I could have asked for, but now her old troubled routine was beginning to get tiresome. But I loved her deeply. Although she was deeply flawed emotionally, there were not many women like her in the world.

When she became pregnant, she wanted everybody to know. At church, she was singing one of the solo parts in an old hymn when she dropped a bombshell from the choir stand.

She was radiant, glowing. Her fingers grabbed the microphone as she yelled almost crudely, "I'm knocked up!" and that set the gossips off. She cradled her baby bump, massaging it in a circular motion, in front of the shocked elders and the astonished deacons. Some of the Mothers' Board, the group of old ladies who always sang off-key, cackled and clapped but some of the other more high-toned members frowned on this rudeness.

"I had to share this happy baby news," Terry said cheerily. "This is my first and it's a blessing from the Lord. Thank you, sweet Jesus!"

Dr. Smart grinned solemnly and shook his head.

Others in the congregation jumped up and down as the organ player did some Jimmy Smith runs on his instrument to accompany her when she shouted at the top of her lungs: "I want you all to join with me in celebrating the new life blossoming inside me. Praise the Lord!"

It was a real emotional roller coaster ride with her. For within that week, she was terribly depressed and swallowed all of the pills she found in the medicine cabinet. We had to take her to the hospital to have her stomach pumped. She fought us all the way. That weekend, she was like a zombie, saying nothing, eating nothing.

The only rise I got out of her was when I said: "Your father has spoiled you rotten. You think everything revolves around you and that is wrong. What are you going to do when you become a mother? What are you going to do when you bring this child into the world?"

She pouted angrily. "Maybe we shouldn't have become parents." Thankfully, the baby was not harmed.

"Why? Do you think they will turn out like you did?"

A chill went through me. I wondered if I had made the right choice of a mate. I thought about whether Terry had the stuff to be a parent, had that wonderful maternal quality to nurture a child. Parenthood. In that instant, I realized what true parenthood meant. How it forced a man and a woman to confront themselves in ways that a person couldn't do when they were alone and self-centered.

"You make my life hell," she grumbled. "You keep on me about smoking too much. I'm a grownup and I can do what I want."

I put a hand on her shoulder. "But you have to think about the baby inside of you. Smoking is not good for it."

She sulked and then reached for a cigarette. "You're not my father."

It was obvious that Terry resisted anything to do with the act of mothering our soon-to-be growing family. She refused to accept the role of wife or mother in this family.

Thinking back to my own mother, Pearl, the type of woman she was contrasted so greatly with Terry. Pearl owned the role of Mama. She was constantly encouraging, supportive, and caring. She made sure that our lives went smoothly. She cheered us on, buoyed our spirits, and made us stronger and resilient even when it seemed everything was going against us. She would do anything for us, the people she loved.

"You don't understand the fact that man was born of woman," she said, making no sense. "That's what trips you up."

"Huh?" I thought we were talking about cigarettes and smoking and pregnancy.

She crossed her legs and fired the cancer stick up. "Just like most men. The only thing you love is that blasted Good Book."

"Please don't smoke, please." I was beginning to get mad.

"I'm a big girl." She laughed. "You don't run me."

I snatched the cigarette away from her lips and tossed it in the ashtray.

"Why did you do that?" she snarled.

"Think of the baby, please," I shouted at her. "I just want you to take care of yourself until you give birth. Then if you want to ruin yourself, go ahead. But the baby deserves a chance, don't you think?"

She was stubborn. She picked up the bent cigarette, which was still lit. "You're like a broken record, like a broken record. If you want to get along with me, please don't repeat things like a darn parrot. My father used to do that. Say something over and over. I hate that."

I put out my hand, palm up. "Give it to me, please."

She took a deep puff, inhaling the smoke into the bottom of her lungs, and blew it out through her nose. "Wait a minute."

"Give it to me, please." She was trying my last nerve.

She did the smoke thing out through her nostrils and then she squashed it out on my palm. The cigarette sparked and sizzled on the tender flesh of my hand. I howled. She laughed and laughed like the bratty kid she was and ran off toward her bedroom.

However, I stopped her by grabbing her arm. She whirled in surprise, her eyes flashing with madness. Her face was inches from mine. I could smell her hot, dry breath.

"You try to be like my old man, my father," she snarled. "You're not a man. He is an uncomplicated man. The only thing that complicates you is your obsession with God, the Bible, and the church. If you didn't have those things, you would be nothing."

I loosened my grip on her. I didn't understand her anger toward the church. Possibly she didn't understand it either.

"My father told me I'd end up in the poorhouse if I took up with you," she said. "And he was right."

She grinned evilly, took off her shoes, and lay on the sofa. "When I married you, I thought you were going to change the world. I was like a wide-eyed schoolgirl. I thought everything was possible. I though the sky was the limit for us."

"And now what do you think?"

"I think you are a loser, just like Daddy said," she said with a chuckle.

"Why is that?"

"Make me some money, make me some bread," she replied. "I want like I did at home. You'll never make money with that God racket. I knew when you started yakking and yakking about Jesus this and Jesus that I was in trouble."

"I want to be saved and live a righteous life," I said. "What is wrong with that? Can you tell me?"

"You used to be fun before you got religion," she said. "That was before you fell under the spell of the Bible. The Good Book killed all of your drive and dreams. My father was right. You are a loser. He warned me about you."

"Before what?"

She reached for the pack of cigarettes on the table. I shook my head but she grabbed it and shook one out. "Life around you is boring. I miss living at home, the swank parties, the costume balls, the galas. My parents loved having people over, but you don't entertain at all. If you do, you have those dull, sanctified clowns from your church over. I hate it."

"I don't have the money to entertain," I said. "We're young and just starting out. We have a baby coming. We have to prioritize. We cannot waste money on foolishness."

She stared at her swollen stomach. "I feel like I'm in prison. I'm young and I want to have some fun."

I smiled. "It's too late now."

She lit another cigarette. Darn, she was hard-headed. I was tired of wrestling with her because I could hurt the baby in some way. She would make me hurt her and I didn't want that.

"I just knew you were the one from the moment I saw you," she said in a strange cadence. "You fooled me. You tricked me with your sweet promises. You lied to me. You misrepresented yourself and told me all kinds of bull. I chose you because you were the least like my father. But maybe you're worse. Maybe I should have married somebody else."

I shrugged. It was hard to get through to her when she was like this. I thought it was funny that she would bring up her father. She had no boundaries with her father. They were like really close pals. They talked about everything, including sex, lust, and romance. She was her father's confidante, muse, and loyal fan.

No subject was too private or personal. There was not a single day that she didn't call her father. Often she called him twice or even three times a day.

Before we went to bed, she could be heard laughing and whispering to him over the phone. I didn't mind that. The thing I minded was they sometimes talked very intimately even when I was in the room. They talked as if I wasn't even there.

I always considered their relationship odd and it crossed the line. But I tolerated it. Once I spoke up about how ridiculously close they were; she blew up in anger and tossed an ashtray at me.

"This is family," she shrieked. "This is blood. You butt out. This has nothing to do with you."

But it did have something to do with me, especially when her father would ask me very personal things. I never discussed matters involving love or sex with anybody, not even close friends.

"My daughter tells me you're lacking skills in the bedroom," her father asked. "What do you have to say for yourself? I'll tell you this. No woman will tolerate some man who cannot perform. What do you have to say for yourself?"

I was sitting in the living room at the time and looked at her. I couldn't believe it. *Some things are private between a man and his wife. How could she?*

"Does the cat have your tongue?" her father asked, baiting me.

Terry had a wicked smile on her face like she had scored points in some kind of evil emotional game. As I walked out of the room, I saw her wink at her grinning father.

CHAPTER 5

CONTENTS UNDER PRESSURE

*Holding faith and a good conscience, which
some having put away, have suffered shipwreck.*
—1 Timothy 1:19

My aunt used to quote Jackie O, the wife of the
sainted JFK, on the importance of rearing kids: "If you
bungle raising your children, I don't think whatever else
you do matters very much."

That quote always made me think. After we had the
two children, Selma and Omar, I wondered how good
a job we were doing with them. I wanted them to show
the values and morals we taught them. To see them
grow up would have filled me with pride and joy. To
see them as adults making their way in the world would
have made me feel like a king.

But Terry robbed me of that. She stole that gift from
me. When she birthed Selma, that moment was the
turning point. We had a couple of kids under our roof,
in a home full of anger, grudges, and disputes, which
was a horrible environment to grow up in.

She was short-tempered. "The kids are making too
much noise. Please do something about them. They're
driving me crazy. I've got a bad headache and I'm
about to wring their puny necks. Please calm them
down. They'll obey you. They ignore me and go on doing their foolishness."

"They're just being kids." I laughed.

"I don't want to be the evil parent but I will," she grumbled. "I get tired of punishing them. I want to be the good parent for a change."

"I don't yell and shout at them like you do," I said.

"That's my personality," she replied. "I don't want to be a witch."

Terry was a good soul. She didn't want to curse in front of them. I thought she was afraid of not being liked or loved, afraid of looking bad. Also, she was afraid of being ignored and losing control. But I knew she got a thrill in spooking the kids. While she treasured Selma, she often punished Omar on a whim. If she was having a bad day, the boy was in for an awful time.

"The kids are getting on my last nerve," she repeated. That was her favorite line.

I knew children need love, attention, and security. She went for days ignoring them, putting on new dresses, adjusting her makeup, or trying on shoes. To make up for this lack, I tried to create loving routines, keeping mealtimes, and helping Omar with his home-work, cutting paper dolls out with Selma, reading bed-time stories, making their favorite snacks, doing fun weekends, and letting them know that they came first in my heart.

Using my mother as my example, I made sure I found time to sit and talk with the kids. I volunteered at Omar's school, counseling other parents and teach-ers. The joy for me was when I saw their little faces light up as I made every birthday and holiday special for them, sometimes over Terry's objections that I was spending too money on them.

Omar was a talented kid. I got him into a special one-to-one tutoring elementary program with emphasis on reading and math. We fought over this matter a lot. Terry didn't think he needed a leg up. I explained to her that competition for slots to one of the better schools was fierce but she didn't want to hear it. We argued over his clothes, shoes, supplies, and backpack.

Often, after a long verbal battle, we would ride in the car in silence. She didn't talk and twisted her wedding ring on and off her finger. I would try to take her hand in mine but she would jerk away.

When we got home, she immediately called up her father and gave him a blow-by-blow account of the dispute. She listened to him while he launched into his anti-husband tirade. The only time I listened in on her conversation, which I regretted, happened while her father was giving her advice about cheating on me. I knew he disliked me but until then I never knew how much.

He told her that she must look out for herself, not sacrifice herself for the kids or our marriage.

I listened to them go back and forth. My brain started racing as I heard my wife talk to him as if he were one of her girlfriends.

"I don't trust myself around other men," my wife said. "I'm so starved for attention and affection. I need a man, any man. I want variety. I'm tired of his softness, his logic, his steadiness. I want to go wild."

Her father agreed. "Then you should go for it."

"Clint makes me sick," she whined. "I feel trapped. I want somebody different, tall and muscles and a deep voice. I want somebody who smells like a man, stinky and husky. I want my body to be tamed and that is something my husband cannot do."

I'd heard enough. This made me want to puke. Her father scheming with her to have an affair, anybody would do, her ex or exes, or even guys in the streets. Just somebody different.

Then Terry started going out at all times of night, supposedly with one of her girlfriends to a club or a bar. Girls' night out. Frequently, I would call her during the day and she wasn't there. She would leave Selma with a neighbor and leave the house and get back just before I got in.

"Will you shut up and listen, Clint?" my wife yelled at me over coffee. "The walls are closing in on me. I'm dying here. Nobody cares."

The school crisis escalated wildly. It went beyond battling over the educational future of Omar, when my wife went up there and acted like a fool. She complained about the quality of the teachers, the quality of the books, and the quality of the children in Omar's class. The assistant principal called me at work and asked me to come up there. I walked with the man through the school, which I found to be very comfortable, and the pupils quite polite and civil.

"Your wife came up to see me the other day," the assistant principal said. "She caused a very big ruckus. She smelled of whiskey. We had security usher her out."

When I got home, I knew better than to talk about her school trip, especially after she began drinking. Omar ratted her out. He told me that she was drinking during the day, tossing them back in front of the television, and got sick in the hallway. I couldn't tell her anything about alcohol. When the alcohol kicked in, she could be a mean, vulgar drunk like her father.

Terry got back at Omar in very subtle ways. She forced food on her child, permitting him to eat himself to a piggy weight in her campaign of revenge. While she berated him about him not cleaning his plate, I tried to keep his calories down. My wife loved sweets, cakes, candies, donuts, pies, cookies, and the like. She filled the boy's pockets up with the sweets. She kept saying something sweet wouldn't hurt him. We fought a lot over this. I knew what she was doing and she knew it as well. She was getting back at me through him.

But Omar wasn't stupid. He realized that something wasn't right with his mother. In his own way, he fought back. Ever the tattletale, he told me at dinner that Mommy had a boyfriend and she talked to him on the phone while I was at work.

"Mommy has a boyfriend, Mommy has a boyfriend, Mommy has a boyfriend," the boy said in a sing-song voice, waving his little arms.

She slapped the child viciously, hard across his face. I grabbed her hand before she could strike another blow.

Before I could restrain her, my wife went into the bedroom, rummaged around in the closet for something, and ran into the bathroom. She locked the door behind her. I held the boy against me until he stopped crying.

I walked to the bathroom door and knocked softly at first, then harder. I didn't know what she was doing in there. She had been acting weird for some time now.

Finally, she unlocked the door. I pushed it open and saw my wife sitting on the edge of the tub. She was staring straight ahead, her eyes red rimmed and fixed. I could see a large vein throbbing in her forehead, which was soaked with sweat.

I sat down beside her. She was holding my gun, a .38 revolver, down by her side. We sat quietly for a time. I kissed her cheek, making her flinch, and slowly removed the gun from her trembling hand.

"Baby, you don't want to do that," I whispered.

"I'm not as dumb as you think or as crazy." She smiled weakly.

"I know that."

She stared at the sink and then at my hand with the gun. "I just need some quiet time. I just want to rest, to sleep, to have some time away from the kids. They drain you and give nothing back."

"Nothing?" I couldn't believe she said this.

She coughed and wiped her mouth. "You don't understand."

"Understand what?"

She looked at me with dead eyes. "You don't understand me. You never did. And I don't think you want to."

I put the gun in my pocket. "Life is hard, that much I know. Sometimes it feels like a puzzle, like a confusing maze, but it will get better."

She frowned and sneered at me. "Please, please, please . . . don't start quoting that Good Book crap to me. Please, not now."

"I'm not. I won't do that. I just want to get through to you."

She was dumbfounded by my campaign to reach her emotionally. "Clint, I'm broken. I wish I could just disappear, just vanish."

"All I want to do is to help you," I pleaded.

"Okay. . . ." Her voice trailed off.

"Did you mean it when you said you get nothing emotionally from the kids?" I asked. "Not even as their mother, nothing?"

"Nada, nothing, zilch." She kept her gaze on the tiled bathroom floor.

I shook my head, and massaged her taut shoulder and heard her purr deep down inside herself.

That night, like most nights, we just lay there in silence with the light on while she leafed through a stack of glossy fashion magazines. However, the morning after the bathroom incident, I found a butcher knife under her pillow. This made me real concerned.

CHAPTER 6

YOU CAN'T LOSE WHAT YOU NEVER HAD

*And he said unto them, Why is ye so fearful?
How is it that ye have no faith?*

—Mark 4:40

My mother reappeared at our home from a long visit to her sister. She was always disappearing when she had enough of the old man's foolishness. The phone call from her after the tragedy was short and to the point. She had never liked Terry, never liked her for my children or myself.

"I never liked her," my mother said sadly. "She seemed to be too involved with herself. You can't be that way when you have a husband or kids. When you have children, you must put those little ones before yourself."

"I know," I agreed.

Her voice became lower in tone. "I never told you this. There was a news report about this car thief in the Bronx who stole a family van and discovered a pair of kids in the back seat. He drove them around but they were making too much noise, so he asked them for their address. He drove them to their home and dropped them off."

"Why are you telling me this?" I asked her.

"Do you know what your wife said? I didn't think much of it at the time. I thought she was just having a tough time at home with the kids."

"What did she say?" I wanted to know.

"Your wife said if she was their mother, she would have made a deal with the thief to keep the little beasts," my mother replied. "She told me she was sick and tired of the kids. And of you too."

"I did nothing to her," I replied. "I always treated her with respect and care. She started staying out late, talking to me like an unruly kid, and wearing clothing that showed off her body like a streetwalker. All I wanted was for her to sit down and talk to me like a man."

My mother frowned at me. "She said you stopped making love to her."

"That's not true. Every time I wanted some, she said she was tired. She always made excuses. I kept on her, asking her questions about what was going on with us, and she had no answers."

"She said you yelled and cursed at her," my mother said. "She wanted to talk with you but you were rude and angry. You didn't let her put her thoughts together, so that's why she turned to me. She was scared. She didn't want her marriage to fail but something had her by the heart and it wouldn't let go. She was in love with this man and he treated her right."

"Like I didn't treat her right?" I was getting really mad. *Why didn't she talk to me?* She went around telling people I was mistreating her and that was not true.

"That was what she said." My mother smirked.

"I waited a long time to get married," I said. "I thought this was going to be the greatest achievement of my life. You know how much I talked about this. I wanted this to work. I thought we could get through any difference, anger, or conflict because we loved each other."

"That was what you thought but she was finished with the marriage," she added. "She felt you were becoming hard and bitter when you thought she was leaving you. You were a changed man. She said she was scared of you."

"Scared of me, why?"

"The last times I saw her were spent with me trying to console her because she was so frightened of you," my mother said. "She didn't know what you would do to her. There was a look in your eyes, like a maniac. A crazy person. Even the kids were scared to see you come in the house."

"Did she say that?" I was confused.

"When she tried to tell you it was over, your marriage, you acted like a fool, ranted and raved. She said you hit the ceiling and threatened to throw her out."

I shook my head. "That's not true."

"I know you, son, you have a hot temper," my mother noted. "You can get really heated up. You lack the skill to disagree without being disagreeable. How could you resolve anything when you fly off the handle all the time?"

I realized I had anger management issues but I really thought that was a thing of the past, some years ago. "My wife knew how to press my buttons. She knew the things that would get me steamed. After she would try to provoke me, I would usually try to change the subject or just walk away when the conversation got hot."

"She said you always wanted to win," she said. "That was real important to you, just like most men. Sometimes making a point isn't worth ruining your marriage over."

I repeated, "That's not true. And you know that."

"You didn't pay enough attention to her," my mother volunteered. "You let her get away. You neglected her and somebody took your place. I know she had her flaws but you should have taken better care of her."

"The devil got her." I smiled a nasty kind of smile.

Now, my mother was not a saint. She left my father for a time when we were kids for another man. It was while my father was further disgraced in the press for selling a property to a developer partnered with a guy who later stole millions meant for 9/11 Trade Center victims.

"I had nothing to do with this gentleman except in trying to sell this property," my father said in a press interview. "I hope my community will permit me to clear my name. I'm the victim here. This shady deal really crushed our financial situation. I know when all of the facts come out that I will be exonerated."

My father was cleared of all wrongdoing but the taint of scandal still stuck to him. I recalled my mother's anger when she stayed with her lover for three years before he died suddenly of a stroke. Then she finally came back to my father.

"Your father was a good man," she said to me. "He didn't deserve what they did to him. He's always had bad luck in terms of life."

Yes, my mother came back but she never wore her wedding ring again. I thought she came back because she had no skills or experience, and needed a man to take care of her. She was once a teacher in the public school system but the city was laying them off. She was the organist, choir director, and minister of music at our church, but jobs in those areas were hard to come by.

With a surprise gift of a bouquet of red roses, her favorite, I came over and drove her to get new glasses. I wanted to continue the talk about Terry from the other day. Thank God, she was still in a chatty mood.

She complained of bad headaches lately and floaters in her vision.

She closed her eyes while we drove there.

"You know, Terry called me a week before she did the horrible thing," she said. "She asked me to come over when your father would be out. I knew this was serious just by the sound of her voice. She sounded anxious, frantic, and on edge. I didn't know what to expect."

"She had just come back in our lives," I said. "I didn't know what she was doing when she was out there in the streets."

"I thought she was getting herself together just like I did when I came home," my mother said. "I didn't leave for the reasons she did. I left my husband, your father, because I was disappointed in him. He had failed me and his community. That's why I left him."

"Why did Terry leave?" I kept my eyes on the road, careful not to look at my mother, who had no real problems telling me what my dead wife had said.

She looked out the window at the people on the sidewalks. "Terry confessed to me that she was having affairs with married men. Only married men. She figured that would be safer than going out with some guy who wanted something steady."

"She knew them in the biblical sense, huh?"

"Yes. There was one guy she became particularly intimate with," she said. "In fact, she was deeply in love with this one and wanted to have his baby. She said she was finished with trying to save her marriage. Her love for you was dead and buried."

"Oh man . . ." That was all I could say.

"She thought this guy was her sexual soul mate, whatever that means," she added. "I told her that passion and lust are not what makes a marriage. It takes hard work, patience, and determination."

"We talked about what it took to have a good marriage before we got engaged," I offered. "I was very serious and I thought she was too. We got all of this down pat when we were in that tiny apartment over on the West Side. Remember that place?"

"That was a dive, for sure." My mother laughed.

"What did she say when you said that marriage was just more than sex?" I asked. "Did she get what you were talking about?"

"Terry never understood that fact," she said. "According to her, her motherhood and wifely duties were killing her. I looked her right in the eye and asked her why she wanted to have this man's baby. That's serious business. Do you know what she answered?"

"No, I don't."

"She said the sex was so good that she wanted to honor it," she replied. "A lot of women do that. That is so foolish. I told her then that I thought she loved being in love and hated when it came apart."

"Terry was strangely romantic. I don't know whether she had it figured out. She was so ruled by her emotions. I think she got that from her father, who is very high-strung. I always hated to deal with him."

My mother pointed to the packed parking lot and directed me to go around to see if there was a space on a side street. We were quiet while the car turned left.

"I think every woman loves the start of passionate love, the kisses and flowers, the drama and the mystery," she continued. "The trick to that love is to sustain it, to keep it alive."

"I wonder why she spilled her guts to you?"

She looked around for a parking space on both sides of the street while she talked. "I don't think she wanted to tell the nasty details of her sordid love life to her daddy. She respected him too much to dirty him with all that she was doing. I know she felt guilty about her actions. She kept saying she was losing her mind."

"The pills weren't working," I said, suddenly confused by all of this. "She told me that. The doctor put her on Zoloft and it just didn't work for her." Her face turned toward me, very pensive. "I think she was in love. I think she was obsessed with him. She talked about getting his wife out of the picture, so she could be with him. Still, she felt guilty about loving him too much but not about having unprotected sex with this guy. After a cruise to St. Lucia, the guy came back and promptly called her and told her he didn't love her anymore. That was a month before she asked me to come over."

I knew now why Terry had started acting so strangely. "She freaked out. It was hellish to be around her. She constantly snapped at me and the kids. She was miserable and wanted to take it out on us. She was always mad. She wanted to make us suffer like she was in her heart."

"When Terry called me after the breakup happened, she was hysterical and almost crazy," my mother said. "She kept saying she couldn't get herself under control. Little things upset her."

"She took it out on the kids," I said. "I didn't mind how she treated me, but I couldn't stomach how she treated the kids. The kids didn't understand what they had done, but they noticed the change in her."

"I told her that I couldn't meet her then and she blew up," she said. "She told me I must meet with her or she would do something drastic. I didn't know I could help her."

"Did you ever meet this guy?"

"No," she said. "I learned about him through her."

"But he was married?"

"Yes. The guy kept jerking her around, saying he was finished with her, then not finished, then he wanted to be with her again. She was going nuts. She told me she couldn't get him out of her system. What she said was her heart hurt so much. Meanwhile, she was mad at you because you were acting like everything was right with the world."

I was stunned. "How was I supposed to act? I had to keep the household together. I had to act like Mr. Mom. When she left, I did laundry, cooked, shopped, took Omar to school, and delivered Selma to daycare. Sometimes I rushed the kids off to bed so I could do my cleaning and write up my notes of the welfare consulting evaluations. I was totally beat."

My mother laughed. "I wish I could have seen you changing Selma's diapers. You always had four thumbs. So clumsy."

"I did okay." I chuckled.

"You asked about the guy," she said. "I know he is a chef. That's all I know about him."

"Young guy, old guy?" I was curious about the man who broke up my family. "Did she say anything about his wife or family?"

"No, she didn't, but she told me he called her at home, which she told him not to do, especially in the evenings," she said. "On one occasion, Omar got to the phone and the little boy could hear music at the other end. She said Omar told you that night. For three days after that night, she put him on punishment."

"She was very hard on him," I added. "They couldn't get along." As another car pulled out of a space, I pulled in, narrowly squeezing into the opening between a minivan and a motorcycle.

There was a softness now in her formerly imperial voice. "Clint, are you all right? You can tell me. I'm your mother, dear."

"I'm good," I said, grinning.

She held my face with both hands, smiled warmly, and kissed me on the cheek. "I'm glad we had this talk. It was long overdue. I knew Terry was not the right match for you. I know this much. Marriage is not what it used to be."

We looked at each other with love. I always thought my mother was a very classy, elegant lady. Her makeup and clothes were always stylish, never trashy or vulgar. I recalled she sometimes dressed up for dinner and at bedtime. Once I saw her in the hallway at night, wearing some racy lingerie and underwear to keep Dad interested. I never understood why my father treated her badly. Maybe he was indifferent toward her because she had left him for such a long time.

Before she got out of the car, she told me I should not wait for her because it could take longer than expected. I didn't know how she would get home. She ordered me to call her that night. Her large brown eyes searched my face to see if her words had caused any damage. Satisfied, she left, closing the car door carefully.

"Weeping may endure for a night, but joy comes in the morning," my mother said calmly as she crossed the street.

I knew that verse from Psalm 30:5, meaning trouble doesn't last always. I knew the cost of the Christian life. My job was to serve God faithfully, no matter what came. I knew God gives us wisdom to learn from the experiences of both gains and losses in this life. God forgives us, God heals us, and God redeems us. I watched my mother walk through the parking lot, stepping between the rows of cars. The thoughts of her revelations unnerved me but I realized I must confront death and reclaim my life. After this, nothing else could happen to bring me to my knees.

CHAPTER 7

FOR A DIVINE REASON

We live by faith, not by sight.
—2 Corinthians 5:7

Shortly after my wife's death, I took up cigarettes again, although I had ended the unhealthy habit over ten years ago. I was never a heavy smoker but the cigarette smoke seemed to calm me. Now, I bought my first pack in years, a box of Camels, the death sticks without filters.

Listening to the sweet tones of James Cleveland singing "Peace Be Still" on a treasured vinyl album, I settled in for the evening. My day job as a welfare agency consultant wore me out. I usually got Chinese take-out, moo goo gai pan or Kung Pao chicken or Hunan shrimp, rather than risk burning up food. The usual fast food was not for me.

The phone rang. It was Dr. Smart, the senior minister at my church. He notified me, his protégé, of the upcoming church retreat at Big Sur, California, where a select group of big-time Eastern Baptist pastors would discuss the future of their churches and the surrounding communities.

"Clint, this is going to be an important conference where you could do yourself a lot of good," the elder pastor said. "Not only will you renew your commitment to your calling, you can chart your course for the future. I recommend you attend."

"I don't know if I can go," I said. Although I took off several days following the tragedy, my supervisor, a heavy-set white woman from Dublin, was making my life hell. It didn't matter that I lost my wife and my children almost three months before. Too bad. She thought I must have driven my wife to her sad end. The harassment had continued almost a year and I was tired of it.

"This is a must event for you," Dr. Smart insisted. "It really is."

Dr. Smart was very perceptive concerning my future, for I knew this was a critical time for a young minister. In my first seven years of my religious service, I served in four different churches, partly due to Terry's restlessness. She couldn't get used to one place. Everything always got old quickly for her. I didn't know how I could make her settle down.

Meanwhile, the elder pledged he would do everything to keep me by his side as his spiritual heir, his shadow, so I could grow with the church. He assured me I would get through this crisis with the Lord's help.

"You know, I've taken too much time from the job dealing with all of this mess," I said, my voice suddenly low. "I can't jeopardize this job. I have too many bills."

"You could borrow from me," the senior pastor suggested. "You could pay it back whenever you get it. Believe me, there would be no pressure."

"No, thank you." I was adamant.

As a junior minister, I officiated at weddings, baptisms, and funerals, unless it was a prominent member of the religious or social community. When Dr. Smart was not available, I comforted the sick and distressed in the church membership of 3,000 loyal followers.

Sometimes I wrote a sermon for the older man when he made a speaking engagement, negotiated with the bickering deacons over their perks, supervised the church bulletins, and even worked with the Mother Board in buying the grape juice for Communion Sunday.

"Why?" the senior pastor asked. "Pride goeth before a fall."

I took a puff on the cigarette and blew the smoke out through my nostrils. Slowly, I directed my somber gaze to the three silver urns containing the ashes of my departed wife and the children. Tears welled up in my eyes but they didn't fall on my brown cheeks.

"Clint, why don't you get a couple of suits to the cleaners so we can do this thing?" Dr. Smart pleaded. "This will do you a world of good. You loved the last retreat over in Pennsylvania. You'll meet people, make connections. I assure you will have a good time."

I sneered, thinking back. "I remember I caught hell from my wife when I got home. She didn't like me being away one bit. She brought that retreat up every time she wanted to get under my skin until she died. It's tough for me to start over. I'm having a difficult time doing it. I know my aunt thinks I should get counseling but I need to do this my own way."

"A loss like you had is never easy," the senior pastor said. "Maybe you should get a breather away from this Gomorrah and go into the fresh air where you can think."

I was quiet, still looking at the urns. I was searching for answers in every holy text: the Old and New Testaments, the Qur'an, the Mahabharata, the Ramayana, the Taoist and Shinto tales and the Talmud. There was no definitive cure. No divine cure. All I had was my steadfast faith.

Dr. Smart cleared his throat. "Clint, everything in this world is all God's plan. Put your life in His hands and you will be rewarded. Just let go and let God."

"I've done that." *Nobody understands how much pain is in my heart.*

The old man was getting testy. "Nobody can tell you how to live your life. See your past for what it is. One of the deacons said you were clueless. I didn't know what he meant until just now. You think this tragedy has robbed you of your destiny and your life. Not true. Don't let Satan rob you of your joy. You've got to take responsibility for who you are. Pick yourself up and stop playing dead."

"I'm not playing dead," I grumbled. "Sure, sometimes I feel like I want to die. God has robbed me of my life. How can I represent Him?"

There was silence at the other end of the line. Then I heard Dr. Smart cough. "When your aunt called me, she said you were just clinging to life by a sheer thread. She was afraid for you. She thinks you're a coward. She thinks you might do something to yourself. I told her that I'd get you straight."

"How do you propose to do that, sir?"

"You're feeling sorry for yourself again," the senior pastor said. "Laugh at yourself and forgive yourself. You've got to learn from this crisis, this challenge. God is testing you."

"If He is, I'm failing big time." I laughed.

"Clint, God won't let you fail," Dr. Smart retorted.

"I guess Prozac, rather than prayer, will provide me with relief," I wisecracked. "Maybe I'm nuts."

"No, you're not. You're grieving. There's a difference. You've had a deep blow to your heart. It will take some time to get over this. It won't be very easy, but you will."

"What do the other members say about me?" I asked, inhaling some smoke. "Do they think I'm crazy?"

"They think you've been hurt beyond belief," the senior pastor explained. "They are afraid for you, just like your aunt. They pray day and night for the Holy Spirit to protect and keep you safe."

I looked again at the three urns containing the ashes of my loved ones. "Dr. Smart, I never thought I could live without them. They meant the world to me. I need help, some serious help. Some days I look at myself and see nothing to like. When my aunt says I'm a good man, I don't see how she could see anything good in me."

The old man was tired of this give-and-take talk. "We can go round and round and round until the cows come home. All I can say to you is this: never let the bad choices of the past influence what you do in the future. Like myself, your life is doing God's work and serving others."

"I guess so," I relented.

"Got to go, Clint, and walk this blasted dog before he pees on the rug," Dr. Smart said before hanging up. "Think about what we have talked about. Really think about it."

Both Dr. Smart and my aunt said prayer was the answer, the perfect cure for my sadness. In the words of my senior pastor, I must bear witness to the Light, I must put myself in a place where I could be still and serene, mentally and physically, so I could listen to the voice of the Lord. Prayer, both of them said, would be the means to fortify my heart and soul.

I got down on my knees near my bed, my hands clasped, in the classic prayer pose. The words to the Divine would not come because the clutter in my mind would not give me peace. It seemed prayer was useless. I had sinned and it cost the lives of those close to me.

O Lord, I find there is no meaning in life. I'm in a rock bottom place and I see nothing ahead of me. I have lost the sense of what I'm here for. How can I search for a way to you? I feel I'm worthless. How can I stand on the shoulders of my ancestors when they have failed me? How can I find the answers to this life unless you reveal yourself to me?

The tears flowed down off my chin. The pain of loss and loneliness was pressing into my chest like a person standing on it. *I work hard but I don't enjoy my life. How can I call myself a Christian? How can I follow the Son of Man and His Word if I am a shepherd and I am lost?*

I pulled myself up from the floor and sat there by the bed, disoriented, out of rhythm with the real world. Although I was awake, not in the deepest of sleep, I thought of a series of biblical images: the burning bush, the Lord's confrontation with Satan, and the divine parting of the Red Sea. Those images gave me comfort.

It was then when I saw my dead wife and my dead boy and girl in a halo of golden light . . . They were beings of glowing luminous electricity . . . almost phosphorus . . . My mind's unruly creation or a holy sign . . . My woman, dead by her own hands, which were covered by dripping blood and the martyred children, whose feet hovered above the carpet . . . featured gashed necks and they were dead . . . The quick sequences of the dream images . . . the illuminated spirits faded into nothingness . . . Their particles of light vanished into a sudden burst of bright radiation. . . .

Shivering, I stared at the wall, not believing that the Lord would speak to me so soon. Maybe it was the devil's work. I was going crazy. I was losing the battle for my sanity. Dr. Smart's suggestion that I serve the ministry without question would help me build up a dwindling faith that would end doubt and fear.

I called the senior minister and gave him my decision. "You were right. We are here to use our lives for greater service to God. I have been selfish. I'm ready to serve the Lord."

Dr. Smart was pleased. "So you'll go to the church retreat in Big Sur?"

"Yes," I replied.

The weeks passed in a blur before I was on the plane to Los Angeles, where I met some of the ministers going to the retreat. At the last moment, Dr. Smart couldn't come because of a family issue. There was a caravan of dark-colored SUVs going to the site, along the picturesque rocky coastline, the sound of the waves, and the vast scenic expanse beyond.

At the site of the retreat, fifty preachers of the Baptist faith gathered at the main building, deposited their luggage, and kneeled in the auditorium in prayer, thanking the Lord for His grace. They sang a few hymns and handed out circulars where the workshops and lectures were listed. Stacks of yellow legal pads were piled on long tables. The pastors discussed which workshops, speakers, and topics they favored, whether their schedules could accommodate their attendance, and the appropriate times for meals and recreation.

The sign above the building read: DAYS OF HOPE AND PROMISE. I stood and watched the group of the religious elite march in and out of the small cottages perched on a wooded cliff. The thoughts of my aunt's urging for a new life and the recent talks with Dr. Smart about my commitment to serving the Lord swirled in my head.

"Ah, the sacred meeting of black men on a holy mission," a pastor whispered to me as I scurried into the building. He smiled in admiration at these men who pledged their lives in service and commitment.

Between workshops, I hiked through the forest, the groves of eucalyptus trees, golden pampas grass, into swarms of monarch butterflies and fields of wildflowers, and along the road leading to the beach. On my walks, I pondered on my loyalty to the Lord and what direction my ministry would take.

The days went by before the weekend retreat. The main speaker was Reverend Hickory Peck, the noted religious firebrand, who guided the 60,000 members of the Strong Oak Community Church in Dixon, Alabama. Very humble, I mingled with the pastors before the address to be held on the closing night of the retreat. I sat in on the various workshops, keeping my mouth shut, smiling when my fellow messengers of the Word scored heavily on the amen meter.

As a young minister, I was torn between the topics of the workshops: The Potential of Christian Youth, A Christian Education, The Future of the Christian Relationship, The Promise of the Christian Community, Lessons in Faith, and Success and Failure of Christian Leadership. When I attended the workshops, I took plenty of notes, participated in discussions, and supported the leaders of the seminars with my energy.

I was totally a part of the gathering, benefiting from the joy and brotherhood of this shared religious life. My soul and spirit were strengthened by the hymns, the sermons, and the collective power of the retreat's worship teams. In that weekend, the force of the Holy Word compelled me to sever my ties to the tragedy, to measure its lessons not as sorrow and failure, but a victory over the struggle of the flesh and weakness.

I was renewed in the deepest part of myself. When I talked to Dr. Smart on a late-night phone call, I was giddy with the redemptive strength of the Holy Ghost.

"Thank you for convincing me to attend the retreat," I said. "I needed this. I was getting into a rut. I was totally lost."

The senior pastor laughed loudly. "I knew you would benefit from the retreat. Your aunt did, too. She's a pretty wise woman. She has learned many lessons in her lifetime. She's not petty, hard, or mean. When I went out there, we talked about you but mostly about her and how she has lived her life. She has lived fully and completely. She knows how precious life is. That's a lesson you should learn too."

"I'm learning it," I replied. "I was so confused. I was lost and too arrogant to admit it. I needed to get my bearings."

Dr. Smart reminded me that God was a loving, compassionate God. But he added God wanted to be obeyed. Nothing more or less.

"Do you think it has helped you deal with your father?" he asked me. "The whole sins of the father thing?"

"I don't know." I needed to think about that.

"I was talking to you about this a few weeks ago," Dr. Smart recalled. "And this was one of your biggest challenges to your ministry. You kept mentioning his calling as a yardstick for your divine purpose. Your father was a very decent man but he was seriously flawed."

"I know that," I said.

I realized many of my current problems stemmed from my childhood years. I rejected the teachings of the Son of Man and everything connected with it. I felt that my people were crazy to believe it for so long, because this religion was not serving them. I was a nonbeliever. Everything went back to the little confused boy clutching my stuffed teddy bear.

Dr. Smart let everything sink into my head. "Clint, if there's something wrong, take your problems to the Maker. Healing can come only from the Lord. "

"I know that too, sir," I said dully. "That's what I'm here for, searching for answers, trying to find a spiritual cure for my problems."

"And you will find one too," the senior pastor replied. "The Lord will remove the fear and pain from your life. He will mend your soul through His healing spirit. I keep telling you this, Clint. Many of us have endured emptiness and loneliness inside, but it can be filled with a loving relationship with God. The Holy Spirit will come upon you and restore you. I know the Lord will revive and restore the defects caused by your suffering and abuse. Clint, you have to trust Him."

"I will, sir," I said. I was tired. I needed some rest. I didn't want to think, just wanted to go to sleep.

"Have a blessed day tomorrow," Dr. Smart concluded. "And safe travels. Get home in one piece."

And the final day of the retreat came. I awoke to the sounds of service coming from the main building across the yard. My body felt alive, almost electric. The talk with Dr. Smart had somehow struck home. I lay there on my narrow bed, listening to the ministers hit all of the right notes of the hymns, their chorus of male voice a mix of Southern sanctified tradition and urban gospel.

My ears were seduced by one of my aunt's favorite hymns, "Don't You Let Nobody Turn you Round":

> Don't you let nobody turn you round
> Turn you round
> Turn you round

Don't you let nobody turn you round
Keep the straight an' the narrow way

I showered, dressed, went out to the dining hall, and got breakfast. It was late. The help said they were shutting down the kitchen to start to prepare lunch. I ate quickly and mindlessly, while listening to the hymns being sung from the gathering in the main hall. By the time I was finished with my meal, the singing had stopped. With my stomach filled, I took my tray and deposited it among the others stacked on a rear table.

Sneaking into the workshop on faith, I crept into the last row of chairs. Brief introductions were made. There was a sense of community and closeness among the members of the workshop. Each of the attendees talked about the obstacles to their faith and practice before the group.

"As a born-again Christian, I don't want to think only of myself," one of them said. "As a Baptist minister in one of the roughest parts of Detroit, I need some life-changing, life-affirming weapons in my faith to battle evil. I want to learn from this gathering and achieve something. Help me, my brothers."

Another reverend confessed as well. "I thought I was all that. I was vain, arrogant, and proud. I thought I was one of God's Chosen, but I'm not doing all that I could do for my congregation. They're suffering while I'm living high on the hog. I'm tired of my old self. I need new ways of looking at the world and new ways of thinking. Can you help me, my brothers?"

This was the New Church. This was a group of ministers, young and old, wanting to serve the Lord by serving His devoted followers. I was so proud of them and their honesty. Hearing the assorted challenges expressed by the ministers, I was bold enough to examine my spiritual drawbacks and explore them deeper than I might dare on my own.

Delving into my deepest feelings was a risk but a risk worth taking. It seemed everything in my life was broken, broken beyond repair.

I stood and addressed the group in a shaky voice. "As a young minister, I have a serious crisis of faith. I have lost everything. I have spent so much time mourning. I have not come out of it very well because I still have so much anger, sadness, and suffering inside me. After I lost my wife and my children, I withdrew from life, couldn't mix with my friends, couldn't get out of bed, couldn't eat. Only now am I starting to come out of this suffocating grief. But I need help. Can you help me, my brothers?"

There was a quiet murmur from the group. The members of the workshop were divided on the cause of my problems, but were collectively in step with the holy cure. I was really pleased for the public catharsis, of telling my crisis to the group. All they wanted was for me to be spiritually sound. That was all.

Afterward, I read in my room. Later, I went to the last dinner held in the great space of the yard, with each of the ministers seated at the long picnic tables there. A group of the organizers catered a heap of down-home food for the pastors: fried chicken, collard greens, fried okra, potato salad, mac and cheese, candied yams, and trays of golden brown cornbread. The dinner was accompanied by polite jokes, small talk, and laughter.

I was seated beside Dr. Hickory Peck, the fundamentalist from Alabama, who worked his charm by drawing the truth out of me.

"I heard you made quite an impression at the workshop today," Dr. Peck said, handling a drumstick. "Some of these traditionalists do not want to believe that a man of God can be tempted. They seem to think if you can speak in tongues or cast out demons, then that is all God requires. Some of them reject the human side."

"And you don't?" I asked.

"No, I don't, but I know all about evil," Dr. Peck said, tearing the meat from the chicken bone. "Do you believe in Satan?"

"Yes, I do."

Dr. Peck grinned. "Satan wants to keep us in doubt and confusion. He wants to bring terrible events in your life so you can choose the road to sin, evil, and mayhem. He wants to keep you under control. He wants to keep you from being happy and at peace, while God wants to heal and cleanse your soul. You must choose."

I drank from the glass of cold cranberry juice. "I have chosen."

"Good," Dr. Peck said, before talking to another minister on the other side of him. Before he stood up, he slipped three cards into my hands. "Read these and when you get back to the city . . . please call. Call me if you need anything. And tell Dr. Smart that I said hey."

Once I finished my meal, I went back to my room. I started packing; then I thought about the three cards given to me by Dr. Peck. Sitting at the small table near the window, I took out the cards and read them.

Faith is a knowledge within the heart, beyond the reach of proof.
> —Kahlil Gibran

To one who has faith, no explanation is necessary. To one without faith, no explanation is possible.
> —St. Thomas Aquinas

You block your dream when you allow your fear to grow bigger than your faith.
                                        —Mary M. Morrissey

I kept reading the cards until I fell asleep. A knock at the door let me know the caravan of vehicles was going to start for the airport. The retreat was over. I missed some of the most important sessions of the event, but the time of quiet and no activity permitted me to think and restore myself. Mechanically, I finished packing my luggage, put the cards in the pocket of my suit jacket, and walked to the SUV.

CHAPTER 8

LICORICE

The Scripture has confined all under sin, that the promise by faith in Jesus Christ might be given to those who might believe.
—Galatians 3:22

Dr. Smart saw the difference in me instantly when I returned from the retreat. The senior pastor thought about increasing my duties as a junior minister, even if it was a slight increase, but he decided to use me as a sort of spiritual troubleshooter. The first person sent to me was an emotionally disturbed male member, who worked as a special assistant to the mayor, a favor as an exchange for political funds allocated to the church. However, the mayor's assistant had been arrested in a brothel downtown. The incident was kept out of the papers and the media.

"Clint, I know you don't do this kind of thing but I need your help on this one," Dr. Smart said. "I've set up an appointment with you on behalf of James Holden. He's a member of this church, but he doesn't come very often. He has some very special problems and I think you can help him with them. This will be a real feather in your cap if you pull this off."

"Why do you think I can help him?" I asked.

"Because of all of the training in counseling," the senior pastor answered. "I know you can do this with that high-toned training from the Union Seminary. Tell me that you will try."

"Okay, I will try." I was very nervous about this favor.

Mr. James Holden, assistant to the mayor, was scheduled to meet with me for a half-hour talk. He missed that appointment. Dr. Smart said, "Clint, you have to keep an eye on him; he's slick." When the senior pastor told me about Mr. Holden, I looked him up on my computer. He was the picture of urban style. A handsome political matinée idol, with a trophy wife, real clout, and everything going for him.

"Reverend Clint . . . You don't mind if I call you that," the unmistakable baritone voice of Mr. Holden said over the phone just before the close of his business day. "I'd like to come over if I could. Something happened to me and I would like to discuss it with you. I think it's important, very important."

"Sure, how about seven this evening?" I said. "At the church."

"Great," Mr. Holden replied. "I'll see you then."

Promptly at seven, the shiny black Cadillac Escalade SUV rolled up and the assistant to the mayor hopped out. He was dressed to the nines, impeccable taste in fashion, Italian suit, and shoes. Tall, lean, and hard body. Licorice colored.

One of the workmen at the building showed Mr. Holden into the hallway leading to the rectory. He crossed the room and shook my hand. Without invitation, he found a seat and immediately lit a cigarette.

"No smoking in the church," I said. "Please."

He put it out on the heel of his shoe, reached up for his kerchief, and carefully wrapped the dead butt in the cloth. "I don't know how much you know," Mr. Holden said. "I am a sex fiend. Can't keep it in my pants."

I was sitting at my desk and showed no surprise. "Mr. Holden, there was some problem over the weekend," I said. "I know about it, an incident involving a brothel and a public disturbance. It's great that you have friends in high places."

He grinned. "Yes, sir. The mayor always jokes that maybe I need a chaperone. I can't keep out of trouble."

"Why is that?"

Mr. Holden laughed again. "Look at me. I'm every woman's dream. They flit around me like honey. And I love sex. Just love it. From the moment I tell her, any woman, to take off her clothes, the game of desire is on. I know how to act around a woman. I know how to charm a woman. I know what they need."

"And what do they need?" I decided to just let him run his mouth.

"Reverend, I make a woman think she is so adored, so desired," the assistant to the mayor chirped. "I give her supreme praise that she doesn't deserve. Women love lies. The man who can tell lies the best gets the most sex."

"Please refrain from those kinds of words," I admonished him.

The assistant to the mayor sat up and brushed a spot of lint on his lapel. "I have had my share of therapy. In fact, the last shrink wanted me to bring in my wife for a family session. No dice. I couldn't agree to that."

"Does your wife know of your problem?"

He chuckled. "She knows I'm a horny dog. I try to imagine my life without women, without sex, and I shudder. I need it too much. I crave desire. I crave lust. I crave temptation. If I could choose the manner of my death, I'd screw myself to death."

"But does she know about your demons?" I ignored his coarseness.

He wanted to evade answering the question. "The mayor says I'll irreparably damage my reputation. The time before last, I was arrested after a night of boozing and sex. The cops pulled me over with a woman passed out in the back seat of my car. I resisted them. Also, the woman was not my wife. The mayor got me out of that jam and now this. This is crazy. This blasted whore-house mess . . ."

"Has this sex addiction threatened your marriage?"

He frowned. "I am always chasing some skirt. Al-ways."

I folded my hands and stared at the politician. "Why are you here? What brought you here? And don't tell me that it was the mayor. Why have you come? If you want to change stripes, we can help you as a believer and a Christian. But if you're just wasting time, then we should let you go on your way. Do you want to change?"

"Yes, I do," the assistant to the mayor said. "I'm scared because I could lose everything I hold dear. I could lose my wife, my health, my home, and my ca-reer. I believe in omens."

"Omens?"

"I picked up a stripper at a club and we went back to her place," he said. "She was so impressed when I told her what I do. The mayor says, 'you can always tell when a broad wants to get laid.' That's just how he says it. Man, it was the sex of the century. There is no vocabulary for what we did in that bedroom. We were in that neon trance where both lose total control. It doesn't get any better than that."

"What was the omen?"

The assistant to the mayor swallowed hard. "After all that kinkiness in the sack, I found a loaded revolver underneath the pillow. I asked her about it. She picks it up and starts unloading it and loading it. She was pretty drunk. She pointed at it at me several times. I got the hell out of there."

"Do you have female friends?"

The assistant to the mayor grimaced. "Sure, I have."

"Other than friends who service you sexually? Other than friends with benefits? Just pals?"

"Yes, I have women as friends," he snapped.

"Do you think you could have sex and intimacy in a loving relationship?"

"This is where the tough questions get asked," the assistant to the mayor said, smirking. "I don't know you that well. I don't even know whether I trust you. The shrink from the clinic kept asking me how many women I had sexually. It was none of his business and it's none of your business too."

I began to lecture him, but caught myself. "Mr. Holden, you fit all of the descriptions under the category of sexual addiction. You are the perfect example of the person who possesses an obsession with sex. Sex is the only thing on your mind. You're indulging in risky sexual behavior, which will have bad consequences on your personal and social life. It will eventually hurt your career."

"So what are you saying that is new?" Mr. Holden asked. "I know all of this already. I'm here to get help. Can you help me?"

"Yes, I think so."

He was adamant. "Yes or no? Can you help me? No Christian mumbo-jumbo. No hocus pocus. I'll do anything you ask, but I need to see results before I self-destruct."

I walked over to the politician, who was getting to his feet. He was taller than me by the length of a head, and put a hand on the elbow of his new spiritual mentor. With a nod of his chin, the assistant to the mayor signaled his departure and left without a word.

After Mr. Holden's exit, I returned to my desk and
flipped through one of the resource books on sexual
addiction. The guy was going to be tough. I didn't know
whether I could convince him that he was ruining his
life. He was hardheaded and took delight in being a
stud. This behavior from the politician indicated a confused mind and a turbulent soul.

I folded a page in the book: compulsive masturba-
tion, multiple sexual affairs, multiple sexual partners,
various one-night stands, constant use of pornography,
unsafe sex, phone sex, cybersex, habitual use of prosti-
tutes, exhibitionism, molestation, rape, and consistent
dating through personal ads.

A call to Dr. Smart was not helpful. He expressed
bewilderment at the politician's ego and arrogance,
and despite the mayor's insistence that the church help
the young man through a rough patch, the senior pastor advised that it might be too late to save Mr. Holden
from himself. He was quite determined to smash his
entire life and everybody in it.

The assistant to the mayor made an appointment on
that Friday after his initial interview, then that following Monday, then that next Wednesday, and then that
following Tuesday in the week after the first meeting.
He kept none of the appointments. He called hours before the times of his scheduled appointments, saying it
was important business and couldn't be avoided.

The phone rang in the early morning hours of Thurs-
day in the second week after the interview. Mr. Holden
sounded very high, almost incoherent. A woman was
giggling drunkenly in the background.

"I got her number, I got her number, I got her number," the assistant to the mayor chanted. "I love some
junk-in-the-trunk. None of them skinny heifers for
me. Love some meat on their bones. Perfume . . . short

skirt . . . a sheer blouse where you can see all of her goodies . . . heavy makeup . . . lips so red and inviting. I can smell her heat."

I didn't find anything funny about what he was saying. "Do you know what time it is? Aren't you ashamed of yourself?"

"No, not really." Mr. Holden laughed. "All I have to do is open my eyes and there is another woman beneath me. See, you don't know about this kind of thing. You don't have the same kind of appetites I do. You're not really a man, are you?"

"Don't insult me, Mr. Holden," I said.

"I apologize for the late-night call but I had to talk to you," the assistant to the mayor said. "I was making a booty call and I said, 'honey, I gotta talk to my reverend.' Yes, I'm a sex fiend. There is so much innuendo and hearsay about me. But it's minor league stuff."

"Sex is not the only answer to life's puzzle," I said. "Only the Lord can make you whole. You've got to address your demons and substitute a healthy, spiritual lifestyle for that old wicked one. Until you do this, you will struggle and fall victim to the temptations of the flesh."

He sneered. "Screwing is what I do. Screwing is what I know."

"No, you're a mess," I said. "An emotional train wreck, really. You need the Lord more than ever."

There was sniffing on the other line of the call. "I cover my head with the soiled sheets and inhale the funk of us coupling. It's a scent that drives me crazy. Just nuts. You know what your trouble is? You're an ordinary man who has nothing to offer life. You're too shell-shocked to live."

"And you are a little boy who is behaving badly," I retorted.

He was a rooster who squawked loud and loved to hear his voice. "I'm a pretty man. The ladies love the deep chocolate color and texture of my skin, the size of my big purple lips, the shape of my flat African nose, and the muscles of my hard body. They get off just by looking at me. Sometimes I see them peeking, checking out my package."

"You and your counterfeit desire," I remarked. "I don't think you like females much. How does your wife like the fact that you are sexually hungry all the time? Does she indulge your freakish ways?"

In the background, the woman shouted in a voice groggy with lust and liquor, "You said you would pay me another two large. I want to see the money. I want to rub the bills all over my body. You pay me and then you can do whatever you want."

The assistant to the mayor said in a hoarse whisper, "You asked for this. I've been married three times. Both of my wives before this one sneaked out on me, met men in hotels and motels, and even the second one used to creep out at night from our bed to be with her lover. I'm not bitter."

"What about your current wife?"

"What about her? She's smart, gorgeous, and sexy. We talk about anything and everything. We talk about our fantasies and sexual experiences. She's more sexually experienced and adventurous than me, if you can believe that. She knows who I am."

"Then why are you doing this?" I asked. The woman with him sounded very young, in her late teens. High-pitched voice.

"Maybe it's performance anxiety, maybe I've been afraid to face myself, maybe I have a marital disconnect. But I know I'm addicted to the scent of woman's flesh and orgasms. I live a double life. I know I pursue dangerous sex outside my marriage. I cheat with hookers and the like. I go to the sex clubs on the East Side and the Meatpacking District. Maybe my wife doesn't pay enough attention to me. She says we should avoid all forms of intimacy because of my sex romps. I don't think she wants to save our marriage."

"Have you ever given your wife an STD?"

The woman's frenzied yelps drowned out his answer. "Give me my money. You promised; then we have all the fun you want."

"Gotta go," Mr. Holden said huskily. "She wants to put her mouth on me." And then he hung up.

After the call, I got down on my knees and prayed for the tormented soul of the politician. I prayed for God to restore the man's life to a sane, healthy place. The next time I was going to recommend Mr. Holden join a Christian support group where he could learn the humility and love as a follower of Christ. I worried that the politician would flame out before he realized what a good relationship with the Lord meant.

Shortly before noon, Dr. Smart called me on his cell phone and told me that Mr. Holden and his young teen companion had been killed in a crash with a cement truck near the exit to the tunnel downtown. The police, the senior pastor added, said the assistant to the mayor was under the influence, as was his passenger, and were killed instantly.

Again, I got down on my knees and asked the Lord to receive the anguished souls of both people into His Kingdom. I wanted to say I failed the soul of Mr. Holden, but I realized it was God's will. I knew there was no room for error in this world. There was a lesson in all of this.

CHAPTER 9

GOING STATIC

*But without faith it is impossible to please Him,
for he who comes to God must believe that He is,
and that He is a rewarder of those who diligently
seek Him.*

—Hebrews 11:6

Dr. Smart assured me that God never believes in
holding patterns. Nothing remained the same for any
amount of time. Life was fluid. I was saddened by the
tragic outcome of Mr. Holden and asked the Lord for
faith, devotion, protection, wisdom, and guidance. I
felt as if I had failed him.

One evening, I was summoned by police to a home
of one of my parishioners. He was holding a gun to the
head of one of his children while his wife and the other
kids looked on. The man had been laid off and was
desperate. He kept waving a pile of bills with one hand,
the unpaid utilities, and the bank was about to take his
house away.

"Let me talk to him," I said to the police captain. "I
know this man. He's a good family man. He doesn't
mean to harm anyone. The strain has gotten to him."

A crowd had gathered in front of the residence, along
with the reporters, police, three ambulances, and just
the curious. It was a circus. I watched the police cap-

tain for approval, and once I got it, strode through the throng to the front door.

"Who's he?" one of the spectators asked no one in particular.

"A pastor," replied another.

I knocked on the door and announced myself, saying I might help the tense situation. Two minutes passed before the door was jerked open. I eased quietly into the living room where I saw the sweating man holding a pistol to the boy's temple. His hand with the gun shook like he had palsy.

"Who are you?" the man asked roughly. "I sent for Dr. Smart. He said he was going to come. Who are you?"

"Reverend Clint Winwood, sir," I replied. "He sent me instead. He's feeling under the weather. He thought I could help."

The barrel of the gun pointed to the head of the boy, who was beyond tears and had wet himself. His mother and the other two children were crouched in a corner in the room, crying and pleading for the disturbed man not to hurt the boy. The man was not listening. He was listening to the angry, bitter voices in his brain.

"I had a good job and could provide for my family," the man said. "I worked for them for fifteen years and this is the payment I get. I put up with a lot of mess. I put up with it for them, my family. They just threw me out. They just threw me out like trash."

I inched toward the man, with my hands out. "A lot of people are going through the same situation. They have lost their jobs and don't know what to do. You've got to hold on. Be strong. Be strong for your family."

"You don't know what you're talking about," the man yelled in rage.

"Yes, I do," I answered. "I know how it is to be afraid, confused, bitter, troubled, and angry at the world. But you have to know that God does not put any more on us than we can stand."

"How can you say that to a black man in this society?" the man asked. "Do you know I was one of the first of our race hired at the plant? The job wasn't much to worry about, it was the white people. I was always under the microscope. They were just watching, waiting, watching for me to screw up. White folks didn't have to go through this kind of mess. Only us."

"I know it's hard sometimes to be black, but that does not mean you ruin your life because people might be stupid and ignorant. You don't have to do this. Not only are you hurting yourself but you're hurting your family. And now you got the police involved."

The man trembled as if he were showered in ice water. "Every day was a different set of insults, slights, and humiliations. Jokes about my race, nappy hair, or the way I wore my clothes. The docs say I got high blood pressure because of this job. I hate this world. Hate it."

Suddenly, the man dragged the boy to the curtains, still holding the gun on the lad, peeked out at the crowd and the police surrounding the house. His eye twitched nervously. One of the other children ran up to the man and begged his father to stop before someone got hurt. His mother walked to the child and pulled him away.

Now, the man and the boy were in the middle of the room. He was furious at the way he had been treated, like a used, abandoned toy tossed out in the garbage. The contorted expression on his face was a portrait of someone going to do something inhuman. He felt desperate and didn't know what he was going to do next.

"I've got my pride, I am a man," the man yelled at the top of his voice. "I don't want to go to no blasted soup kitchens, food pantries, or emergency shelters. I got my pride. I played by the rules. I deserve a decent life. I worked hard all my life."

I moved slowly toward him and stopped when the man turned to face me. "I know you have. You seem like a hard worker and a decent family man. But this situation can only end badly, not just for you but for your family. You don't want to do this."

"I worked hard all my life," the man shouted. "I don't want no relief. I don't want no food stamps. Or some meaningless low-wage job. Picking up trash, scrubbing toilets, sweeping up sidewalks. I got my pride."

"So this will solve everything?" I asked. "Shooting your son is going to make everything right?"

The man slumped as if the air had been let out of him, momentarily lowering the gun from the boy's head. "I can't afford to keep up my mortgage. I went to the bank and they won't help me. I don't want to be homeless."

I knew it was now or never. I really wasn't concerned about my safety; I was thinking of the boy and the tragedy that was about to unfold.

Instantly, I tackled the man, gripping the hand with the gun tightly, allowing the boy to run. We sailed over the sofa, landing solidly onto the carpeted floor, where the gun went off. His wife screamed shrilly. The shot went through the wall, its booming sound echoing in the small room.

His wife sprinted to the front door and let the police in. We were rolling around on the floor, kicking tables over, and smashing against walls when the cops separated us. They immediately jerked the man to his feet, handcuffed him, and led him to a squad car.

"Don't hurt my father, please," one of the children said, crying.

I got up with the assistance of one of the patrolman, staggering, but intact. "I don't do this very often." I smiled. I walked with a slight limp, with the cop holding me up.

The cop looked me over. "You're going to have to see about your face. Your eye looks pretty bad. You're going to have a shiner in the morning."

The man's wife mouthed the words "thank you," and kissed me on the cheek as I went to depart. She knew the situation could have had a different ending, a much sadder ending.

"You got a fan there." The cop winked. As we exited from the home in the middle of the street, applause could be heard in ripples around the block. Some of the neighbors patted me on the back and others shook my hand. A reporter tried to interview me but I chose to sit for a moment in the rear of a police car to collect my thoughts.

Another lesson learned. God is good.

CHAPTER 10

PURE TENDERNESS

My brethren, count it all joy when you fall into various trials, knowing that the testing of your faith produces patience.

—James 1:2–3

On that next Sunday, I was treated like a hero, a warrior priest who had made his mark out there in the real world. It really helped that I was interviewed by media, on television and the radio, and many church blogs spoke reverently of me. I stood there on the stage of the church next to Dr. Smart while he applauded my worthy achievements as a bold man of the Word.

"Don't let that praise go to your head," Dr. Smart said later. "People can be fickle. They cheered for me once and now they think of me as an old war horse soon to go to pasture."

"I don't think of you like that, sir," I replied, touching my bruised eye.

The old minister loved my humility and that I really didn't take myself too seriously, although all the adulation would have puffed up the head of any insecure young man. The brashness of the overconfident youth, Dr. Smart reasoned, had fallen away with the loss of my wife and children. God was retooling me right before his eyes.

"I have another favor to ask of you," Dr. Smart said, patting me on the shoulder. "I'd like you to see this woman who has a world of trouble. Maybe you can help her. She has lost her faith, much like you."

I smiled. "I'm healing bit by bit."

Dr. Smart told me the woman would be coming in to see me late afternoon after dropping her grandmother off at one of her friends'. He warned me to go easy on her, but he avoided telling me what her specific problem was. Perhaps he didn't want me to prejudge the woman.

However, the old minister added there would be a call from one of the workers from the State Department of Children and Families, briefing me on the case. It was a most difficult case. Sure enough, the call came into my office from the worker, Miss Hudson, responsible for the case of the woman, Dionne Willis, the thirty-eight-year-old mother of twins, DeMarcus and DeOwen. Both were eight years old.

Miss Hudson said Dionne Willis was a victim of substance abuse, on welfare, and had birthed the twins with drugs in their systems. The state was taking her kids away because it was felt that she could not provide a proper home for them.

"If you need any other information about the case, feel free to call me," Miss Hudson said cheerily. "By the way, I saw you on the television. That was a brave thing you did. A lot of people would not have done what you did."

"Thank you very much," I said. "Did you make a visit to the house, to see where the children were staying?"

"Yes, we made a visit. We showed up without warning to see the real home situation. No appointment time. But we found the house very clean. Spotless. The problem is not with her parenting skills but with her drug problem."

I was curious about her addiction. "Is she still using?"

"No, I don't think so," Miss Hudson remarked. "However, everyone is afraid of a drug relapse with her. We wanted to get the kids out of there into a safe environment. The action was ordered because the woman was a client on assistance and one of her sisters tested positive for PCP. Better safe than sorry."

"Will she be able to get her children back?" The thought of losing one's children was a familiar one to me. The loss of the kids was a heavier burden on me than the death of my wife.

"No, they have been placed in a foster home," she replied.

"Is there no way she can reverse this process?" I asked.

"No, unless a formal review is considered," Miss Hudson replied. "Thank you for taking the time to see her. We will speak later."

I sat at my desk, peering out of the window at a group of kids bouncing a ball. I wondered why Dr. Smart assigned this woman to me. There were three other novice ministers in need of seasoning.

When the appointment time arrived, a woman, mocha colored, dressed in a gray business suit, walked into my office, all smiles. She appeared younger than her age. Introductions were made. The woman sat on the sofa rather than the leather chair near the desk. She crossed her long legs seductively and watched me for any response. I didn't give her any. This was strictly business.

"What can I help you with?" I asked.

"Dr. Smart sent me to you," Dionne Willis said. "He said you could help me make sense of the situation I'm currently in. I was a drug user and got in trouble with the law. But now I'm clean. Still, the state has taken my children away. I'm at my wits' end."

I looked at her intently. "I talked to one of your social workers. She filled me in on your case. The safety of the children, she says, is their biggest concern. She was worried that your home might be dangerous to their health."

"Bull crap," Dionne Willis snapped. "Did you talk to Miss Hudson? That hussy doesn't like me at all."

"Why?"

"Reverend, I did everything they said to do. All of the visits, all of the interviews, all of the paperwork. I know I messed up in the past. I was young and wild. I screwed up my life. I messed up but the kids shouldn't be taken from me for good. They need me. Another worker said Miss Hudson just had a grudge against me and made sure that the kids got taken away. That witch . . . I don't think this is what God wants for me, for them, but for some reason, He burdened me with this obstacle."

I remembered the story in the news where a four-year-old girl remained with her family and was reportedly sexually assaulted and ultimately killed by her stepfather. *Why did they take the twins out of Dionne's home? Is there more to this story?*

She watched me with a passive face. "Does God really care about us? Will my suffering ever end? Tell me, Reverend."

"Yes, yes to both questions."

Her expression transformed into one of utter anguish. "Don't lie to me, Reverend. I asked God for help but He turns a deaf ear to me. He never hears prayers from poor folks. He simply just don't listen to us or hear us."

"Not true," I disagreed.

"Furthermore, I think God is for the rich folks. He lets us suffer without any relief. All we have is God and nothing else. That's not good enough. Look around you. That's all poor folks have. I think our life's purpose is to suffer for all of the sins we've committed or are about to commit. I have suffered all my life. And now my kids are suffering. That's not fair."

"Sometimes life isn't fair," I suggested. That was what my aunt used to say.

"Be honest, Reverend," she said. "How can I pray and be heard by God? Does He hear me?"

"I know He does," I said. "He's led you to here. That's something."

Without missing a beat, Dionne Willis covered her face and sobbed like a movie heroine, heartfelt but polite. She dabbed at her puffy eyes. It was obvious that she had been crying earlier, before she came here.

"I carried them," she moaned like a good girl. "Now I've lost them. There's a void in my heart that time will never heal. When the worker took them away, the kids stirred up a ruckus, trying to get out of the car by clawing through the glass of the windows. Crying and stuff. They wanted their mama."

"Yes, they did." My voice had a soothing tone.

"The witches at Social Services did this to me," she hissed. "They were talking about adoption. No way. When the worker led them away, I thought I was going to die. I kept thinking, *I'm their mother, I'm their mother, I'm their mother.* I couldn't just walk out of their lives."

"What evidence did they have?" I asked.

"The state investigators interviewed a neighbor who said I slapped my little boy in public," she said. "Said I slapped him hard in his face, on a bus no less. She was just pissed at me because her old man was flirting with me. Then another neighbor said I punished the other boy without letting him eat and had him sitting on the porch crying his eyes out. That's crazy."

"Hearsay?"

"I never did that, Reverend," she said. "They slander single moms. They think we're all streetwalkers. Hookers with welfare checks. People know me know that ain't so."

"The worker who called here said there is a series of abuse reports," I countered. "Two or three came over the state's hotline. I don't know if you had a relapse but something was going on at your home. When I looked over your report, the school noted that your son De-Marcus bore the marks of a brutal beating on his little arms, legs, and backside. They said the welts appeared to be caused by an ironing cord."

"That's unthinkable," she protested. "I would never mistreat my children. Never. Whoever says that is a liar."

She continued her plea with a tug on my sleeve. "Reverend, please don't let them do this. Please don't let them take my babies away. If I let them do this, I won't be able to face myself. Please."

Dionne Willis went into her purse and handed me a photo of two bright-eyed toddlers, the twins, in all their Easter finery. They were a picture of civility, fine breeding, and everything that is good with babies. She said her boys were almost four years old when their picture was taken.

"Don't give it back, keep it," she said. "When you think about this case, look at those babies and think what is best for them. They need their mother. They can give me all this psychobabble about a mother in recovery and her kids but I would never hurt them."

"Probably not intentionally," I replied. "But I will look into this and give you a call."

After Dionne Willis left, I thought about all of the people who were having hard knocks and felt their hope and faith were gone. I knew life could be full of contradictions. What I didn't want to confront was the issue of whether the state should be able to lift the kids from her home. Was she essentially a wicked person? Or a backslider?

In the parking lot, I talked with one of the workers at the welfare agency and she explained how poverty worked and how it traps people in its web. I was more fortunate than most. My family was solidly middle class. The woman explained that Dionne Willis was a welfare queen, relying on unreported income, off-the-book jobs, and generous boyfriends.

"Some people cannot let their children go hungry," I said. "They'll do anything to stop that. I can understand that."

"Or maybe some people should not be parents," the worker retorted.

That night, I found a note about the power of prayer written by the disciple John, reminding me:

No matter what it is that we ask according to His will, He hears us.

I set the photo of the kids next to the note about prayer and thought about the inner pain of a mother without her babies.

The second session occurred because Dionne Willis wanted it to happen. She said she was in the neighborhood. She strolled in, well dressed, a bad wig on her head, and a cup of coffee. Before she took a seat, she started talking about her childhood and a recurring dream of her drowning with a wall of outstretched hands reaching out for her in a fog.

"Do you know how my husband died?" she asked me.

"No, I don't."

"I lost my husband at the beach over six summers ago," the woman said. "We were waist deep in water, splashing around with the swimmers, when the water just pulled us down. The riptides took him away from me. He was never found."

"I'm sorry," I said. "That must have been a great loss."

Again, she flipped into the raw throes of rage. "I'd kill the witch if I knew where she lived. I'd hunt her butt down and kill her. She's the devil. She took the only things that mattered to me in this life. She ruined my life."

Her cell phone rang and she answered it. She turned away from me so she could have some privacy. Her whispers were annoying but I tolerated it. She got up, not giving me any explanation, and left.

Probably I was too close to this one. I needed to look at my feelings. I talked with the worker and she was adamant about Dionne Willis not getting her children. She was pushing the adoption angle and was lining up a nice family for them. The children needed love and affection. Dionne Willis would lose her kids. This was not an unresolved issue.

Dr. Smart never crowded me when I entered one of these matters. The senior pastor let me do my job. The old man knew his young charge would be thoughtful, compassionate, open minded. I would never label any of these folks sick or abnormal. The lessons gained through the hardships of these people taught me about myself, how to look into their souls, what I could offer the person in the way of healing, what I could do to put the weary soul back on track. It was not about success or failure. Talking to them honestly provided relief for both of us.

Still, I realized I must keep an emotional distance from their problems. The emotional force of the conflicts would suck me into a vortex of morality, ethics, judgment, and madness. Often, I thought about whether there was any such thing as sin or vice. Maybe it was what people did in their natural state. Like the Bible said.

A week after our last meeting, Dionne Willis called and ranted about the worker and the adoptive families and her lost children. She screamed again about the Lord forsaking the poor folks, that money was what mattered, and this society was built on that golden rule.

"I'm at the end of my rope," she shouted. "I'm going nuts."

"Why do you say that?" I asked.

"One of my boys, DeOwen, called me from the foster home and said he was miserable," she said. "Said he wanted to come home, said he misses me so badly."

"When was this?" I asked.

"A few nights ago," she replied. "And my other boy, DeMarcus, is giving his foster parents hell. He keeps banging his head against the walls until his nose and ears bleed. They are really worried about him. When they returned him home from the hospital, he tried to cut his wrist with a razor blade. He wants to come home. The woman stopped him."

"Did you talk to the worker on your case?"

She mumbled a curse word. "She said I was going to lose them forever. She said I was not a good mother. She said I was trash. She said she was going to send me to public housing. The projects. Dag her."

"I'll talk to her again," I said firmly. I knew she would be a tough sell.

Her voice drifted off. "Sometimes I go in the kids' room, lie down, and just look at the ceiling. I cry and cry and cry. I'm mad all the time. I'm mad at God. Why did He do this to me and my boys?"

"The future is not hopeless," I said quietly.

"But I have some good news for you," the woman said. "I'm pregnant. I told her that I was and she said the state will move to take this one away from me too. Just as soon as I give birth."

"How many months?" I was stunned.

"Two, that's all." She giggled. "Isn't that great?"

I put the phone down and shook my head. This was a new wrinkle, as if things weren't bad enough.

As soon as Dionne Willis concluded the call, I walked straight to Dr. Smart's office and confided everything about her case. I was amazed that the woman would get pregnant while trying to fight for the rights to keep her children. "What bad judgment," he said. We put our heads together to concoct a plan to give her a partial victory.

"We must get around the more hurtful aspects of this case and look for the positive," Dr. Smart said. "Remember the truth can be subjective. Maybe we will go to the worker's supervisor to ask her for a formal review of the case. I know the woman is a high risk. But maybe we can find support for her as a mother and a parent."

"What about the new baby?" I asked. "She couldn't lose anymore. She has lost enough. She'd probably go off the deep end. She really would."

In the next few days, we took to the phones, first to the agency administrators, second to lawyers, and then to a state representative who owed the old man a favor. An agreement was hammered out among the state agency, the mother, and the politician who changed the mind of the worker's supervisor.

"How does it feel to get to keep your new baby?" I asked. "I know it's not what you wanted. I know you wanted your twins back with you but at least it's something."

She snarled on the other end of the line. "Maybe it's for the best. I wouldn't want them back if they didn't know me. They'd treat me like I was a stranger after all this time. Maybe it's in the best interest of the kids."

"What about your new baby?" I asked her. I talked to one of the outreach staff at a local hospital who said it was very difficult to be a poor woman tackling the mother instinct in this modern world. She joked, saying the poor ones probably could benefit from a dose of Prozac.

I disagreed. Sometimes prayer could be more effective than analysis or Prozac.

"This new baby is a new lease on life, a second chance," Dionne Willis chirped. "I got a new man. I like him. We talked and cried. We hugged, kissed, and said we had each other. We whispered about love and commitment. And, yes, we went to bed early and tried to make us happy."

"And you accomplished that feat," I said, laughing.

Afterward, I opened the Bible and read the following passage from Job 34:10: *Far be it from the true God to act wickedly, and the Almighty to act unjustly.*

That said it all.

One more lesson learned. Don't get uppity because He is watching us.

CHAPTER 11

PAPA DADDY'S BACK

Yea, and if I offered upon the sacrifice and service of your faith, I joy, and rejoice with you all.
                              —Philippians 2:17

During the rise of my spiritual career, I attended an event at one of the neighboring churches, agreeing to deliver one of the addresses to welcome the new members into the fold. A collection of four churches gathered there, assembling the sainted elders and veteran brothers and sisters, as well as the new souls. I walked among them, this future of the spiritual fortresses in the community, and greeted some of the people who had known me since I was a young boy. My dress was casual and the mood on the park grounds was light and easy.

Everyone, all of the big shots of the churches, gathered under a striped canopy at the edge of the park, with a large silver cross as a backdrop. There were two platforms for the choirs and the musicians.

"No, Dr. Smart cannot come but he sends his regrets," I spoke to three of the deacons of the Temple of Revelations Pentecostal Assembly and the St. Paul's A.M.E. Church.

"We'll miss him this year but I hear you're doing great work for the Redeemer," Deacon Douglas said.

"You've truly become a warrior for the Lord. Remember the whole community is watching you."

"I know that," I replied. "I try to do the good works."

Deacon Garfield interrupted. "Did you know your father is over there? You should go and surprise him. He doesn't know you're here. You can't miss him. He's holding court as usual."

I looked around to the group of boys and girls tossing balls around, the smaller giggling kids chasing balloons or coming down the slide, and the grownups sitting in clusters on the picnic tables. His voice boomed from a gathering of the more prominent church officials, making his opinions more convincing by the loud sound of his words. My father didn't like to mix with the lesser church members if he could avoid it.

As I neared the esteemed group, I hear my father saying to the men: "We had so much hope that Obama would be different but he has not done anything for the black folk. We're worse off than we were under Bush. None of the young black men can get a job and that is hurting the community. No black woman wants a man if he cannot love, protect, shelter, or nurture her. He's worse than anything we could have got from having a white man in the White House."

I interrupted his tirade. "Wrong as usual. President Obama is doing his best trying to clean up the mess that Republicans put us in."

"Ah yes, young blood . . ." My father turned and put his arm on my shoulder and guided me through the crowd. "Let us go over here. I want to talk to you."

"Okay." I walked over to a tall, sturdy oak tree and leaned against it. My father waved to some people he knew, grinning like he was running for mayor.

This was going to be one of those macho talks again. My mother stressed how I, as a black boy, walked in the world, while my father emphasized winning, beating the odds, and coming out on top.

"Everything's messed up, not just your life," my father started in on me. "I heard you talked with my wife the other day. I advised her against seeing you. I told her that she was going to stir things up in you, things that you should forget."

I knew every time my father came in contact with me that there was going to be some talk about fatherhood, romance, and parenting. In the talk, there would be something negative about me and how I conducted my life. I never asked him for anything. I didn't see my father much. He was off doing the Lord's business. He provided money to put a roof over our heads, fed us, and paid the bills.

He scowled at me. "You always blame other people. You blame Terry. You blame your parents. You blame me. You even blame God."

"What are you saying?" He was always putting me down.

He folded his arms and glared at me. "Son, you think you're special. You're not. Most of these black boys aren't. Brothers have been catching hell for as long as time has existed. It's nothing new. Life is hard."

"I don't want anybody feeling sorry for me," I said defensively. "Nobody, not even you. I'll make it my own way. I don't need your help."

He waved again to more people, who were members of the other church in the old neighborhood. His full attention was now on me. "Don't get me wrong," my father went on with venom in his words. "I don't mean to be rude, but I don't like you too much, son. You're everything I wouldn't like to have in a son. You have all these people fooled. They think butter wouldn't melt in your mouth, but I know who you really are."

"And what is that?" I was beyond rage.

"You're a loser," he said acidly. "You're a chump. I heard from my wife everything that Terry did to you. You deserved it."

I shrugged. I was shocked by his verbal slap.

"The bottom line is you're a weak man." He could be very cruel and sarcastic. "You're a loser. You forced Terry to do this terrible thing."

"Who do you think you are talking to?" I wasn't going to back down.

He smiled at me. "Clint, my son, I think you're a stuck-up, pompous loser. You've lost everything. You lost your wife. You lost your kids. You lost your family. Now, you've lost your self-respect, your pride, and your faith."

"You're wrong, so very wrong," I said, my voice breaking. "I still believe in love, marriage, and family."

"Your mother said I should show you some support, some compassion," he said. "She said you have had a horrible tragedy. I'm supposed to pamper you like a girl who has lost her doll. Well, I can't, because no son of mine is going to act like a sissy. Be a man. Grow up."

I used to admire and respect him. I used to worship him as a man and a father. He possessed all the answers, even when he was wrong. He was God.

"Dad, you're a stupid fool," I said slowly. "You're so full of yourself. You mistreat everybody with ignorance and meanness. Look at how you treat my mother and my sister. You treat them like dirt."

"You can't speak to your father like that," he barked, his face an angry mask. "I won't tolerate it."

"Why don't you act like a father should?" I was tired of him.

"Thank God, the kids were killed before you could mess them up any further," my father growled. "Omar would have been a punk just like you."

I resisted punching him in his mouth. I remembered Omar, my little prince, in the last days before the murders. He was having temper tantrums, crying a lot, and just acting out. It was like he could sense what was about to happen.

"You were making Omar into a chump just like you," he added. "I knew you were making him a spoiled brat. He was too darn soft."

I recalled when I was a kid. I was real quiet, very shy, scared to speak up in class. One of my teachers wrote a letter to my parents and the old man let me have it. He told me I was a disgrace to the family name. A little punk.

"Clint, we couldn't be more different," my father said. "You're a sissy. You're a loser. God blessed you when he took your family away."

The last time I saw my father was on television, shouting at a heated early-morning hearing protesting the Port Authority's planned toll and fare hikes.

His supporters were behind him as he stood on a chair so he could be seen.

"I'm sick of being taxed," my father yelled. "These hikes are a tax, another tax on us, the working class. You're lining your pockets at our expense, you fat cats, and we say we have had enough. Our budgets cannot take it anymore. We're sick of paying for everything. When are you, the rich folks, going to pay for something?"

The clapping drowned out everything he said after that. My father loved the attention, being the center and focus of everything. He thought his very presence took all the air out of a room.

Now, under this oak tree, I was telling my father what I thought about him finally. "What you can't face is that you're an old, bitter, cruel man," I said somberly. "Dad, your race has been run. You're finished."

"Son, you will never measure up to me, never," he gloated.

When my father said that, I realized the clock of life was ticking. He really dreaded getting old. I never understood why the young were so impatient to grow older. I shook my head and walked away toward my car.

CHAPTER 12

A MATTER OF SELFLESSNESS

As the body without the spirit is dead, so faith without works is dead.
—James 2:26

I awoke the following morning and set about cleaning my apartment, cleaning the bathroom, taking out the trash, scrubbing the floors, polishing the furniture, and washing the dishes. Taking a break from the routine, I watched the news on television: a water main break downtown, a liquor store robbery, the assault of a city councilman's wife, and a celebrity vixen wearing no underwear while getting out of a limo in Las Vegas.

One of the deacons called and told me about his brother mowing down a woman crossing a busy Midtown street. She was pushing a baby carriage. The tot was unhurt. The brother lost control of his car, smashing into a series of vehicles along the road before pulling to a stop.

"Can you go to visit him at the city jail?" the deacon said. He had a reed-thin voice, much like the man who played Barney Fife on the TV's *The Andy Griffith Show*. "He won't let us visit him. I think he is ashamed of what he has done."

"Yes, I will see him," I agreed.

That next morning, I went to see the deacon's brother at the lockup. Any visit to jail or a secured place always jarred me. The brother was a medium-sized man in an orange jumpsuit, prison regulation, walking slowly in shackles. He was accompanied by a guard, who directed him to the visiting room, a small cage with wire mesh over the windows.

"Hello, Reverend," the man said while sitting down. "My brother, the Holy Joe, told me to expect you."

"Hello, Mr. Burke. Your brother said I could do you some good," I replied. "Do you want to talk?"

Mr. Burke looked down around the room, its emptiness, the wire mesh over the windows, then at the guard. "They say I killed a woman. I don't drink. I don't use drugs. I don't listen to music. I don't watch TV or movies. I don't do anything."

"How did you get in here?" I asked him.

The eyes of the deacon's brother were sad and empty. "You know, when you leave school, you think you're going to change the world. You think everything is possible. But you quickly understand you're just a small ant in a bigger anthill."

"Why did you end up in here?"

He pulled up the chain with his military dog tags from under his T-shirt. "I got hurt in the war, in Iraq. A car bomb wrecked my Humvee in Baghdad and my head got smashed up pretty bad. I've got an iron plate in my head."

"How long have you been home?"

"I was a Marine corporal," he said warily. "I was a war hero over there but now I've hit rock bottom. Shrapnel went into my body and nothing has ever been the same for me since. I have anger management issues. I get mad too fast. I got plenty of counseling from the VA but it doesn't help. I wake up and everything starts spinning. I take pills, lots of pills. They don't help. I sit around the house, moping, in a funk."

I wanted to know what he did to land behind bars. I was interested in his past, but the present had the most appeal for me. "Would you say that the incident about the dead woman is a pack of lies?"

"No," Mr. Burke answered. "I did what they said."

"What happened?" I asked.

"We've been arguing over finances and medical bills," Mr. Burke said absently. "My wife wants us to keep our arguments behind closed doors but when I fly off the handle, I go ballistic. My son, Donald, asked me why do we fuss and fight so much. He said he thought we were fighting over them, our children. One of my daughters, Melissa, tries to break up our arguments. She gets in the middle of us."

"What happened that day of the incident?"

He stared at the guard, who watched us intently as we sat at the table, monitoring every glance, every move. "Things got crazy. After several arguments, she locked me out of the house and took up with another guy. This was the first time I've drunk liquor after my discharge. I needed to get out and breathe fresh air. I went to a bar and drank too much. But I didn't know how alcohol would affect me."

Sometimes people tended to exaggerate or withhold facts when they're were in a crisis. Mr. Burke told me what happened, with his lawyer filling in the gory details. I knew what occurred on the street involving the intoxicated former soldier and his hapless victim, the car smashed into another car and another car and another car and then hit her, sending her and the carriage flying. Luckily, the child in the stroller only suffered cuts and bruises. I imagined the onlookers screaming and yelling at the speeding car pulling off down the street, trying to get away.

"I could see the people running out to help the woman after she was hit and sprawled on the pavement," Mr. Burke said sadly. "I felt the car pass over her, heard her shriek, and she went down. The papers said the witnesses told the cops that she wasn't moving, bleeding from the head and mouth, and looked like she was dying."

"Did you see her walking across the street?" I asked the prisoner.

"I ran four red lights and lost control of the car," the man in shackles replied. "I blacked out. I lost control of the car. I didn't want to kill her. I hit another car on a side street and fled. I ran away and wanted to keep running. I didn't want to kill her."

"What now?" I questioned.

Mr. Burke looked stunned.

"What?"

Now, the voice of Mr. Burke quivered as he wrung his large hands. "My family loves me, and my wife and I love each other. My kids want me to come home. I used to feel sorry for myself. Not anymore. I know what I did. My family kept telling me that I was in complete denial. I thought I could work this through. It's the war, the war. Darn, I could have dealt with my problems a long time ago."

"How do you think it's affecting the children?"

His sad eyes glistened with tears. "My son wets the bed. My two girls get bad grades in school because they never speak up."

I reached into my coat and retrieved a copy of the Bible. Quickly, the guard walked over to the table, took the Holy Book, and shook it out. He leafed through the Bible's pages, checking for weapons or other illegal items.

"Okay, here," the guard said, handing the Bible to Mr. Burke.

"Sometimes I feel like a sucker, a patsy, a fool," the prisoner said. "The country screwed me. My wife screwed me. I'll take whatever is in the cards. I don't know what's going to happen. I still believe in the system and I'll take whatever it says is my fate. I'll be strong."

I placed my hands over those of Mr. Burke's and said a silent prayer. I closed my eyes but the woman's killer's remained open.

"Everything started with God and will end in God," I told Mr. Burke in a serene tone. "It's not about you. Nor has it ever been. The purpose of your life is not about your personal achievement, your solace, or even your satisfaction. You exist only because of God's will. It is only in God that you discover your meaning and your purpose and your destiny. Remember that when you say your prayers."

"Is that it?" the prisoner wisecracked. He was still feeling sorry for himself. Not thinking of his wife or the children.

"Yes, that is it," I concluded.

Walking out of the city jail, I took a deep breath and thought of one of Dr. Smart's frequent sayings: "Without God, life makes no sense."

I called the deacon that evening and told him that the visit went as well as expected. Mr. Burke realized his fate was sealed. He knew he was going to get a harsh sentence for killing the woman, a wife and a mother of a young child. The elders often told me that we are destined to fail during this life, that we cannot always measure up to the standard set by the Lord. *I know this is true. We all know that. We are all sinners.*

CHAPTER 13

SPEAK EVIL

But the Lord is faithful, and He will strengthen and protect you from the evil one.

— 2 Thessalonians 3:3

Her parents brought her in. They called their daughter Miss Beelzebub or Sister Lucifer, nicknamed her after the Great Deceiver. They considered her evil personified, a dark, fallen angel, a wicked serpent.

They considered her a troublemaker, a liar, a practitioner of impure thoughts and deeds. They promised the cops that they would get her help after her latest stunt misfired. Sister Lucifer went berserk and trashed a room at a New Jersey motel. When the motel's manager opened the door, he discovered everything was in total disarray, furniture overturned, mirrors broken, the TV smashed, and the bed with a slightly burned mattress. A young teen boy, completely tattooed on his chest and arms, was knocked out in a corner of the room. There was a strong smell of crack.

Following his inspection of the room, the manager noticed the girl, now nude, running across the parking lot, screaming and waving her skinny arms. The police officers were forced to Taser her after she resisted them, before they got her into the squad car. She was drunk, high on drugs, agitated, and bit one of her captors in the brief struggle.

Katherine, also known as Kat, sat on the sofa next to her parents. They seemed mentally fatigued after the motel episode, but as members of the church, they didn't want to lock her away in one of the state mental institutions.

"Reverend, they say you can do wonders with the hard cases," Kat's father said. "Now, my daughter has a record. She's been fingerprinted and photographed by the police department. I warned her before she ran away from home. I don't want her trapped away in some padded cell in a local psychiatric unit. Please help her."

"Talk to her, Reverend," Kat's mother pleaded. "She's not a bad girl. She just got mixed up with the wrong people. She got mixed up with those druggies, pimps, whores, thieves, and perverts. After she ran away, she worked in a topless club and massage parlors, and became a nude dancer in a strip joint."

I saw Kat's lips move a bit, as if she was struggling to say something. I stared at her mouth, coated with black lipstick. Although she wore a long fake fur coat, the cold weather did not prevent her from wearing a sleeveless top, revealing her midriff, and a short skirt. She was coal black in skin color. Her hair was pulled back and blond.

"I don't believe in shrinks," Kat intoned. "I don't believe in mental hospitals, I don't believe in doctors, I don't believe in pills, I don't believe in pastors, either."

I sniffed the air. Kat smelled like she had not had a bath in several days. She seemed as if she was "self-medicated," like the TV reality shows called it. I noticed the gold pendant, L'Homme, around her slender neck.

Her father ignored the funk and pointed to her shrunken face. "She used to be so pretty," he said. "This is how she looks after living on the streets for over two years and selling her body."

"I knew you were sexually active before you turned sixteen," her mother added. "I sneaked a peek at your diary. Smoking dope. Doing other illegal drugs. Drinking. I was appalled by those entries about how you were messing around with all of those older guys. Seven, eight, and nine of them."

"I'm not a whore," Kat hissed.

"You act like one," her mother asserted. "You act like a stray cat."

I asked the daughter with a passive smile, "Do you have protected sex? You don't want an unwanted pregnancy."

"Heck no," Kat shouted. "I'm a teenager. A lot of teen girls do it. We get into situations that get out of control. But I control my life."

"Yeah right." Her father smirked.

Her mother leaned over to the girl and said in a soft voice, much like a loving matriarch, "Baby, then why are you so sad?"

The girl laughed harshly. "This remark shows you how much you know about me. You don't know anything about me."

"This is the kind of nonsense we have to tolerate with her," her father said. "She needs to take her medication. The voices in her head would bother her less. She's changed. She has a potty mouth."

"She wants to run the streets to act like a tart," her mother added. "That's why she's so, so sad. I agree with my husband. She needs to take her meds."

Kat grinned like a maniac, clowning for me. "My parents think just because I'm sad, then I must be depressed. One doesn't have anything to do with the other. If I was really depressed, my parents would know it and I would too."

I watched the interaction between Kat and her parents, observing them like an insect with a pin through it being studied by a lab attendant. I realized the daughter was in emotional pain, and her parents were in complete denial. There was more to their girl than classifying her just as an out-of-control kid. Everyone was at fault.

"Happiness irks me," Kat continued. "The reason I left home is I got tired of my folks telling me that my choices had consequences. I got tired of them telling me that I was grounded. I'm grown. I needed to be on my own."

"Do you believe in God?" I asked the girl.

"I don't know," Kat admitted. "God doesn't give a care about me."

Her mother screamed at her like an infidel who never knew a measure of divine grace. "You need to come to the Lord."

"A good life does not mean you live as a good Christian," the girl said nastily. "Christians as a species have messed up everything on earth. They are small-minded, selfish, and have no conscience. Christians are responsible for a lot of the misery on this planet. Christians are savages. They destroy everything they touch."

Her parents shuddered. "Talk to her before she becomes lost and ends up in hell," her father said, turning to me.

"It's like my daughter was abducted by aliens," her mother noted. "Where is the sweet, shy little girl who used to carry around her stuffed toys? Where is my baby who had the cutest smile?"

"That girl is dead and buried," Kat wisecracked, sticking out her studded tongue.

"Shouldn't you worry about your soul or your sanity?" her mother asked her. "You have made yourself a total disgrace. We can't show our faces in public."

The father looked a little miffed. "The docs say it's schizophrenia. Nobody has anything like that in my entire family. A fruitcake. How can she go to college? Nobody will have her in their school."

"Maybe you've always been a mental patient right from the start," her mother said coldly, then turned to me. "I don't know how much you know about her. My daughter's first hospitalization happened at age eleven. She was talking real crazy. She said she imagined me with my arm chopped off. She said she imagined an army of rapists stalking her. She said she imagined her father burning up in a pillar of fire in a crowded street. Just nutty talk."

I watched Kat, who appeared tired, her face drawn and chalky. She was rocking back and forth on the chair, humming something. I felt a pang of guilt. Her parents wished she didn't exist.

"Mommy, you were abusive," the daughter said in baby-like tones.

"Kat's second hospitalization occurred in middle school at age fourteen." Her mother sniffed, ignoring the girl. "A total emotional collapse. She was taken away, swearing, screaming, delusions, hallucinations, the whole nine yards. I wanted them to treat her with electric shock or a lobotomy, but my husband, the gentle soul that he is, refused to do that."

Her father piled on in the verbal slaughter. "Remember, dear, when she kept calling her art teacher, calling and calling and calling and hanging up. He wanted to press charges but we talked him out of it."

I was truly concerned about the girl. I wanted to see how far her parents would go in the mental demolition of their daughter. They said they were here to get some answers. Her father even mentioned how he tried to bribe her into good behavior with some cash and a brand new car. That didn't work.

So now it was tough love. The burnt earth approach.

"Don't let Kat fool you with that sweet look," her mother said. "She lied, she stole, she slept around with a crowd of older guys, she ran away many times, she used drugs, she pulled a knife on a student. Don't let her fool you with her butter-won't-melt-in-her-mouth expression."

"You treated me like puke," Kat said. "You treated me like trash."

"Girl, you know you're lying," her mother howled. "You accuse me of being abusive. We have bent over backward to give you everything you wanted. No other parents would have treated you like that if you had caused them so much trouble."

"You treated me like garbage," her daughter repeated.

I watched her parents shake their heads in disbelief, while her mother angrily said her piece. "Kat, you know I never did anything like that. I didn't strike you or call you bad names or tell you that you were worthless. Honey, you were nasty to me and very rude to your father. We cannot tolerate that. Cannot."

Her father frowned. "Katherine, you're pathetic."

The harsh explanations of her mother undermined the fragile girl's self-esteem, and allowed her no breathing room to defend herself from her aggressive parents. She told me how her daughter caused so much commotion in her household when she sliced her wrists right at holiday time.

I could have sworn I saw the girl flash a coy grin, then look away for a second. Again the mother listed her offenses: cutting school, no bathing, drugging, drinking, and shunning all personal hygiene. She added that she knew that her daughter needed help, that the time was running out for her intervention.

"I'm sorry I caused so much trouble, Mommy," the girl said with a sarcastic edge to her voice.

Her father taunted her. "Do you want to be listed as an emotionally disturbed person, handcuffed and locked away in the loony bin for endless psychiatric evaluations? Do you?"

"I think that is enough negativity for now," I suggested.

"Reverend, do you believe that I'm loco?" the girl asked me.

My gaze was direct and alert. I stood up. "I think I need to talk to Kat alone. Can I ask you to go out in the hallway for a few minutes while we talk in private? Please?"

The parents glanced at one another, shrugged their shoulders, and left the room. Her mother looked back with a frightened expression as if she was afraid for my life. When the door was closed, I moved from my desk to the sofa next to the foul-smelling girl. I knew a young woman in crisis when I saw one, a lost soul with emotional needs and unresolved issues stemming from mental illness.

I watched Kat breathe a sigh of relief. "Thank you. I don't think I could have taken too much more of that barrage."

She closed her eyes and sagged back on the sofa. "The voices inside my head keep telling me to do things . . . things I should not do . . . They would tell me to do things and I wouldn't know why I did them . . . All that yelling and moaning from my mother only makes it worse . . . I have my highs and my lows . . . My thoughts seem to race . . . and sometimes I get these high-energy rushes and it's hard to relax . . . Can't sleep . . . Can't eat . . . then I drink too much and too often . . . or do coke . . . and do something stupid . . ."

I kept my voice very low and very calm. "Kat, sometimes parents mean to love a child, but they drop the ball and get caught up with their lives. I think your mother doesn't understand you nor does she know you. A lot of parents have that problem."

"Tell me something, Reverend," the girl said.

"I don't think they realize how ill you are," I added. "They're dealing with you as if you're a normal young woman. You have special challenges and special needs."

I knew the problem now: this was a broken young woman with an outlaw adolescent type of attitude toward her life. She wasn't going to address her issues by shrinks prescribing tranquilizers and antidepressants, trying to overwhelm the torment of her emotional pain. She needed more than that.

The girl ran her shaking hand through her hair. "I'll toot my horn. I love it when people talk crap. I know, self-esteem does not come from parents. Reverend, don't preach at me with the fire and brimstone jive, ok?"

"I will try to not bore you." I grinned at her.

"I feel like I'm a failure," she moaned.

"No, you're not," I said. "Don't live for your parents. Live for yourself. Invest in your life. Change your approach. Change your direction. Those are the things that will regain your emotional and spiritual health."

"I have tried my hardest to turn things around," she replied.

"Keep trying," I said in a peaceful voice. "Kat, believe in your own worth, your own dignity. You matter, you count."

"Madness is the aura that surrounds me," she said in a sing-song tone.

"What does that mean?" I was puzzled by her non-sense.

Her eyes narrowed into menacing slits. "Sometimes I want to kill myself. Sometimes I want to kill somebody. Sometimes I want to die. Sometimes I have crying jags. Sometimes I really do feel like I'm crazy."

"You've got to fight Satan," I countered. "You have to chase those crazy notions out of your head. Find your center of peace. Find that thing that comforts you. "

"How can I?" she pushed back. "I'm anti-life. I'm anti-family. I'm anti-God. Believe me, I won't miss this miserable life."

"You're talking foolish," I said without a blink.

"How can I believe in God or the Bible when it is all a fairy tale?" she answered real hard. "They are myths for the people to feel good about the emptiness of life. They are as fake as Bugs Bunny or Felix the Cat or The Simpsons."

I waved her off, interrupting her thoughts. "Your parents want the best for you, but they are so busy trying to keep a roof over their heads. They are preoccupied and you crave their approval and affection. They are busy with the business of their own lives. Don't fault them."

"They can't change me," she assured me. "I'm a stuck-up hussy."

"These are indeed surface things," I said slowly.

She shifted into a sexy, feminine pose. "As long as I can remember, men have been telling me how beautiful I am," she said sensuously, licking out that spiked tongue. "Everyone says so. Women too. It's strange. When I look in the mirror, I don't see what the fuss is about. If I think like they do, I'd forget I'm human. Even my mother says I could be a fashion model. Shoot, my life feels like a movie script."

"Kat, do you enjoy being a woman?"

"Sometimes," she cooed. "One of my mother's girl-friends told her that I had white blood, mixed, pitch dark with white features. This one man told me I look Cuban. Another said I look dark Ethiopian. Men make me feel like I'm a freak. Everybody loves sexy black curves. Men like the way I carry myself. Some of the witches, though, call me a slut or a tart. I love being the rogue hottie."

"Why are you talking like that?" I chided her. "Respect yourself. Respect your womanhood."

"I notice that black men are more talk than action," she blasted back. "They talk a good game but when you ask them to put up, they fold or wilt. Boys will be boys. As you're talking about respect, remember Rev that I'm the underdog in this little sick drama. I'm fighting for my life."

I focused all of my attention on her, now speaking in deliberate, hushed words. "Even I cannot cure your pain. Only you can do this. You cannot blame your parents for all your life. You must do something for yourself. Be honest with yourself. Try to be a reasonable human being. Be realistic. The pain is not going to go away in two seconds. You might have to endure this confusion for the remainder of your life but let people help you. Let someone into your life."

"Do you believe that?" the girl asked.

"Yes, I do," I answered.

She laughed. "I wish I were a man sometimes."

"Everything will heal in time," I said. "Both your mind, your spirit, they will heal. It'll get better."

Her hands covered her face, making her words muffled and odd. "Reverend, I hope when I die that the spirit doesn't go on for too long. I want death to be just sheer emptiness. Darkness. Nothingness. Like it is before you push your head out between your mother's thighs."

"It will not be. That will be the day of judgment."

She sat stone-faced, but her response was immediate. "Bull."

"The Bible says, 'we will stand before God one day,'" I replied.

"Do you really believe that?"

"Kat, you keep saying you're a failure, you're a mistake," I said. "God had a plan in creating you. It has nothing to do with your parents. God's plan adjusts for lust, sin, ignorance, intolerance, and even evil. What you must understand is that God does not create failures. God does not make mistakes. He does not create accidents. There is a reason He created you and you have to find that purpose."

"So you're saying forget about my parents, it's about me and God," the girl replied. "Now, you're making sense."

"No, I'm not saying disrespect your parents," I said, focusing on her and making every word count. "I'm saying your life should be about finding God's purpose for you and you alone. Your job is to make God proud. Living for God's glory is the greatest victory you can achieve with your life. See, when anything in creation fulfills its purpose, it brings joy and celebrates the glory that is God."

"There is hope for me yet," she said. She gave a shy grin.

I smiled. "Let God have His way with you."

We remained silent and in deep thought for several seconds. The session was a grueling one. I listened to all kinds of bad words and bad ideas. Confusion is a hard enemy to defeat, for the person can wrap his heart, his soul, his spirit in it. I would follow this initial session with others and insure that Kat would have a fighting chance. I knew there was more I could and must do to deliver her soul to salvation and redemption.

"Can I hug you?" she asked me. "You're a good man, Reverend."

I did not want to ask on what she based that conclusion, but I stood and held the girl in my arms. Her tears rolled down her pretty face and she clung to me with a fierceness that I recalled in the tender moments with my children. It touched me greatly.

"Go ahead and cry, Kat," I said. "You're safe now."

When I called her parents back inside, she was sitting on the sofa, calm and collected, with her hands folded. Her mother looked at her strangely. But her father shrugged and walked to the window as if mesmerized by the snow.

"There is no devil in this girl," I said forcefully. "There is no evil, no devil in her. All she needs is care, kindness, and a bit of attention."

"Like heck," her mother muttered under her breath.

I invited them to pray. Everyone knelt in place and stretched out their hands to the other. I spoke a healing, serene prayer, with all of the proper clauses for protection and wisdom.

One thing I noticed was Kat's blazing eyes widening and suddenly I found myself confronted with the full impact of her evil, damning stare.

I thought, *Oh Lord, this is going to be tough. Saving souls.*

CHAPTER 14

HOME COOKING

Be on your guard. Stand firm in the faith. Be men of courage. Be strong.
— 1 Corinthians 16:23

All of the elders reminded me that He was a loving God, but I must fear His judgment and wrath. He would pick up the pieces in my life, but I must trust Him. I must expect the best. I must take risks and confront life's challenges head-on.

I continued my unending campaign of prayer. Prayer heals. Still, I was lonely. I sat on the sofa, listening to a college basketball game on the radio, with one of my favorite teams getting blown out. The thought of my destroyed family troubled me greatly, because Dr. Smart often hinted I was at fault for the disaster. And maybe I was. But maybe I was not supposed to take responsibility for someone's choices. Terry made that hateful choice.

Often, I knelt down and spread all of the photos of my slain children. My fingers traced the features of them, remembering their noisy shouts, the running through the house, and the full-throttle energy of their young bodies. To be honest, I was surprised by how deep loss and grief could go. Many people had died before in my life and I experienced a strong sense of sadness and loneliness, but nothing like this. There was a big hole in my heart.

This kind of grief was so crushing and painful that sometimes I had to fight for breath. Every other night, I awoke in the apartment, eyes almost swollen shut, with a horrible ache in the center of my chest. Often I'd call my church members or even my coworkers with a faltering, tear-strangled voice, but they didn't know what to say.

I tried not to indulge in self-pity, feeling sorry for myself. *Nobody knows the utter depths of grief and regret.* I kept telling myself to steer clear of wallowing in that dark feeling. As a minister, I knew life changes in an instant, in a heartbeat, in the sudden flash of a passing thought.

Grief is a living death. Sometimes I'd stand with friends or coworkers and then the pain of grief would swallow me like a black cloud. It would come on me in crippling waves. At work, I'd run through the halls, pushing past people to go to the lavatory and cry my eyes out. The worst times were the funerals; even my friends and the church elders doubted I could get through the ceremonies. Once it was over, I fell apart.

Why did Terry do it? Why? My family saw it before I did. I thought marriage and the kids would change her. I was mistaken.

At first, we were so much in love. I couldn't tell where she ended and where I began. *What went wrong?*

I recalled Terry saying, "I have a long, long track record with men. You're not the first. Treat me like I know my way around the track. Okay?"

What causes a marriage to come apart?

During our third year together, I became worried about our marriage. I knew my wife was slipping away from me. The fact was that I was guilty of saying nothing when trouble arose and letting things fester until a real crisis occurred. I didn't challenge her. Terry wanted attention and I didn't give it to her. She kept saying I worked too hard for the church.

She also said my good work would never get noticed. I hated it when she said my work always made somebody else look good. Like Dr. Smart. Maybe she was right about all of it; maybe my work got little appreciation.

Winter never lifted a person's spirits. A grating music sounded from the scraping of the snow and concrete as the city plow tried to weave in and out of the parked cars. I listened to the noise and reached for my warm green tea. But the voice inside my head spoke up.

My wife should have walked away from this marriage, this family, because I stopped giving her what she needed most: love and attention. The status quo was too painful. She knew I was not going to change their life around. The church and God came first and everything else second.

The deal breaker for our marriage was when I turned completely to the Lord, I removed her from my heart. I became a total control freak. The church was everything. Still, my wife stuck around because she believed that the future would be much better than the past. Most women were like that.

"You never let me work out my issues," Terry once said with a frown. "I had postpartum depression, the baby blues, both times when I gave birth. You didn't even notice what I was going through."

"Yes, I did," I said. "I knew something was wrong. I just didn't know what. And you were not talking. You just kept your mouth shut."

My wife snapped at me savagely. "You never cared. All you cared about was the church, kissing this one's backside, kissing that one's backside. What about me? What about the mother of your children? What about your wife? What about your children? We always came in last."

"Why didn't I stay at home with the babies?" I roared. "I had to earn something for us to live on. I know it was tough. You were so lethargic, didn't care about anything, either our babies or yourself."

"It didn't take a genius to figure out that I was depressed," she countered. "Why didn't you care about us like you did for those folks in the street? Or at the church? You should have taken care of home first."

"I did," I replied angrily.

"No, you didn't," Terry snapped.

The phone rang. It snapped me back to the present. The memories of Terry and our busted union fell away with each ring.

Lisa Reynolds. It was another church member, a woman who had one of the most pressing of problems: a missing child. Last Wednesday, she was in the frozen food aisle, fingering the cold boxes of vegetables and fish. She was a regular customer at this local supermarket. Once in line, she asked a woman to watch her toddler girl so she could go back for two cartons of orange juice. Just three minutes.

In the time it took to get the juice, the little girl was gone, vanished along with the woman, and the police said the pair was seen walking from the store to a late-model Dodge. The authorities suspected her ex-husband as the culprit behind the abduction, yet he offered an alibi of being in the Midwest on a visit to his ailing father.

"Can I trust these white folks to do the right thing?" she asked me.

"I don't know why not," I replied. "They're police and FBI, so there should be no problem. They will find the baby. I know it."

"Should I call the press to get some publicity? Go on the TV or something."

"That might backfire," I answered. "What do the cops want you to do? They do this kind of thing every day."

"I don't want my baby hurt," she insisted.

I curled up on the sofa, cradling the phone against my face. "After you reported the baby's disappearance, what did the police do? Did they search for the toddler? Or did they tell you to wait?"

Her voice cracked with emotion, a blend of sadness and sorrow. "One of my girlfriends came and took me to the hospital. I was hysterical. I was out of control. They treated me for shock and gave me a shot."

"But what did the authorities do?" I insisted that she answer the question. It was like everything was a blur for her. How long had the baby been missing before she notified the police? What took her so long to act?

"They searched all around the area, some three thousand people, combed the area all the way to the highway and on toward the airport," she said. "They had all kinds of people out there: employees from the textile plant, some workers from the afternoon shifts at the mall, firefighters, forest rangers, cops, Boy Scouts, a group of Masons and Elks. Everybody."

"And nothing turned up?"

"Not even a clue," the woman said. "Now, what I called you for is to ask you to go down to the police station with me on Friday afternoon and fill out the missing person's papers. I need you with me."

"Do you have any family who you could call?" I asked.

"No." She was emphatic.

"Did they completely check out your former husband?" I wanted to know if he was involved. She appeared still shaken by the event.

"Yeah, the snake said the baby's disappearance had nothing to do with our getting broke up," she said. "He said he couldn't stay with me because of my temper. He was gambling. He was always at the casino or playing the horses. We were going through a rough patch before the baby got snatched."

"Is that true?"

"Yeah, it is. Can I count on you to go with me? I would be lost without someone there with me. I get nervous around cops."

"You can count on me to go with you to meet with the police," I said confidently. "I'll call you that morning and we'll figure a place to meet. Or maybe we'll just meet there at the station."

The woman cheered up. "That's good with me."

As soon as I hung up the phone, there was another call. There was a downside to the notoriety gained from my heroics with the hostages. Everybody called to get my help. Now, the call was from an older man with a reedy voice, much like a flute or a piccolo.

"Reverend, we need your help," said the man, who introduced himself as Mr. Lloyd. "Your reputation precedes you. The community needs your assistance. Maybe we can use you to rally the people around to the issue of saving our young people."

"What part can I play?" I asked.

"There is a meeting tomorrow at Dr. Smart's office at four," Mr. Lloyd said. "He volunteered your services as a representative to the schools, civic groups, and churches around the city. He says you can be a most effective advocate. Also, we need the families, the parents, the communities to be involved. There is no parental guidance. The kids have no mentors or suitable role models. They need more concern, love, experience, and wisdom."

"That's true, Mr. Lloyd," I agreed. "I will make that meeting."

"Let me finish, Reverend," Mr. Lloyd continued. "If we don't get to the bottom of this crisis, then the kids will get involved in the criminal justice system and really present a grave danger to our society. We have too many of our young men and women there already. We can't throw these young lives away. We have the opportunity to intervene."

"You can count on the church," I said. "Yes, I will be there. I will always do my best for the kids."

That night, I stayed up, reading Bible passages and bits from Dr. King's essays and sermons, *A Testament of Hope*. One thing I realized was the important role that the black church played in the spiritual nourishment of the community. The ministers were often out front on the social and political issues. It was a responsibility that I welcomed.

I read a note, written by Dr. Smart, tucked in the book. A few months ago, I loaned Dr. King's book to the senior minister and had not looked inside it when he returned it.

Faith is taking the first step even when you don't see the whole staircase.
—Rev. Martin Luther King

The following day, I approached the meeting expecting nothing. Mr. Lloyd spoke the truth about the social needs of the young people, but I hoped there would be more solutions than rhetoric. *Talk, talk, talk.* Often, I attended meetings and conferences, served on panels, where nothing was accomplished but promises and more promises to remedy the youth crisis.

Inside the office, Dr. Smart was joined by Reverend R. K. Arenas, Mr. Lloyd, and another man, who kept silent during the entire meeting. I observed and kept notes in a small black book. Mr. Lloyd welcomed me as if I were a long-lost brother, shaking my hand, then hugging me. However, Reverend Arenas just nodded at me in acknowledgement. Cool, clinical, and calm.

"Let me thank you for coming out in this weather," Reverend Arenas said. "We know what we are up against, this deadly epidemic of bloodshed and wanton violence. Our youth, especially our young men, are killing themselves at a record rate and we are being robbed of a most precious resource. Our community is turning to us, the church, for help."

Mr. Lloyd, a thin man with a fashionable suit, interrupted him. "Some say this carnage in our poor neighborhoods is killing our future. The nearby communities are racking up an estimated dozen funerals a day from the violence and drug-related causes. We must do something."

"But what?" I asked them.

Reverend Arenas, cocky about his esteemed position and physical appearance, straightened his tie and said, "Well, young blood, the church must go beyond just saving souls and preaching to their members. It must go beyond ministering to the smug black middle class. It must venture out into the inner city and get its hands dirty."

"Sounds like we're missionaries in darkest Africa." I sniffed. "I go out into the community without any limit on class or gender. That's what we are supposed to do."

We laughed, except Reverend Arenas, who frowned at my sarcastic statement. Quick to keep the peace, Dr. Smart put his finger up against his lips in a signal to hear the arrogant minister out.

"We must move fast to halt this bloodletting in the inner city," Reverend Arenas said firmly. "We cannot fall back on what we have already done and complain about not filling our pews when there are trying times in our community. We have much work to do. The goal of saving our young should be the only thing we hold as important and that should be the thing that unites us."

Dr. Smart, ever the wise elder, leaned toward the men. "And I believe that God will help us move toward that goal."

"But how do you get all of the churches on the same page?" I asked. "We cannot agree on anything in the matter of Christian outreach. We still consider the people in the hood as mutants, freaks, and mistakes. The poor are sinners and we should minister to them, period. If they go down, then the whole community goes down."

"Careful, careful, Clint," cautioned Dr. Smart.

Mr. Lloyd agreed with me. "The young man is right. The church must fulfill its role as an important agent for social and cultural change to be a leader in the issue. The church cannot fail. It is our only hope."

That set off Reverend Arenas in an angry torrent of words. "The young reverend has a point. However, there are some class differences in our community that cannot be overlooked. Historically, Jim Crow compelled us to live collectively in one area. The white world roped us off in rigid geographical, political, and social boundaries. They made us live together. When the Civil Rights Act passed, the professional community got out of the neighborhood, taking the middle class with them."

"What are you saying?" I asked.

"I'm saying that the middle class came from poor backgrounds but their dreams and aspirations were middle class," Reverend Arenas countered. "There is no common ground between the black middle class and the poor except for the color of their skin. The middle class and the poor have nothing to talk about."

"I don't agree with you at all," I said, taking offense to that.

"Furthermore, the black middle class wants the same things as the white middle class," Reverend Arenas replied. "They don't want to be around the poor. They want to get away from the poor as far as possible. Young reverend, you want the best for your children. You want to see them prosper and thrive. You don't want to see them poor. There may be only so much the church can do for the poor."

Dr. Smart held up his hands, trying to signal the men to curb their aggression. "Reverend Arenas, the children of our young minister are dead, so go easy on that. Please respect his loss. Still, I don't know if I share your view. The church has to step up and do our work."

My stare was penetrating and lethal. "I'm sure that the Lord wants us to reach out to everyone, not a select few. The Lord is not that shallow. He does not mean for the church to neglect the neediest, the most troubled, the most neglected. Sure, we cannot expect the government to do everything. We must save our own young men and women. This is something we must do."

"That's madness and you know it," Reverend Arenas said, meeting my stare. "The church protects its own. The church is not going to stick its neck out, only to get it cut off. Yes, the Lord knows we must spread His Word but He understands the church is a business. He knows the poor have nothing to contribute, nothing whatsoever."

To break the impasse, Dr. Smart pointed out what his church was offering in the fight to end crime and violence in the community, by mentioning counseling, job training, and rite-of-passage sessions for young black men at risk. The mentoring program, under the senior minister's guidance, allowed church elders to work with troubled youth, instilling a new sense of pride and self-worth along with traditional training.

"Do some of the young people have criminal records?" Reverend Arenas asked. "My church would not let that element in our building."

"Yes, many of them do," I admitted.

Dr. Smart explained that several churches were forming a coalition to increase services in their programs for at-risk youth in the worst areas of their communities. He tried to convince the arrogant minister of the value of the prison ministries and the community patrols which had closed eight major crack houses and converted four of the buildings to low-income neighborhood housing.

"The church has to say yes to these people who have always heard no, no, no," I said. "The church has been the only place where the poor and the troubled have been able to see their lives have worth and value. Fully. Unconditionally."

"If we continue doing this, this crisis will split the church into divisions," Reverend Arenas argued. "The church will survive even if we have to cut some of those in the community off. It will always survive. It will always endure."

Mr. Lloyd shook his head. "But we sacrifice the poor."

"What is the point of this meeting?" I asked.

"We're arguing over something that no amount of time or energy will resolve," Reverend Arenas replied.

"The poor are lost with their lust, vice, murder, and ignorance. They are cutting their own throats. They complain about the white man. He is not doing this to them. They are doing this to themselves."

"This was a waste of time," I said and invited Mr. Lloyd to walk out with me. We left the office with Reverend Arenas still lecturing about the immorality of the poor and how the Lord does not expect more of them than their base animal nature.

CHAPTER 15

SOULSVILLE

*Be thou faithful unto death, and I will give thee
a crown of life.*

—Revelations 2:10

I was still shaken by the audacity of Reverend Arena's assertion about the role of the church in the lives
of the poor. However, many of the church's followers
felt this way, ignoring the historic foundations of the
mighty African American religious institution that
propelled the race to equality and triumph. I was completely disappointed in how the meeting went.

During the at-risk meeting that afternoon, I gathered the dozen young souls around in a circle, with
me in the center of it. These were the kids everybody
wanted to abandon. None of them are gangbangers or
thugs, but troubled nonetheless. I usually wore a dark
suit for these young people, but I now decided to pursue a casual presence. Most of the youth in the group
were black teens, mere boys who had no idea what the
world was about. For some reason, the number of girls
were very few.

"Do you know what Henry McNeal Turner or Rich-
ard Allen accomplished in our history?" I asked the
teens.

One of them yelled, "Allen plays point guard for the Celtics. I know him. Good three-point shooter."

"Turner sang with Mary J. Blige at the Dick Clark's New Year's Eve bash they have every year," another shouted. "Had a tune with rapper Kanye West and Drake. It dropped last month, right?"

"No, wrong, wrong, wrong," I said.

"Are they politicians or professors?" one teen yelled.

"No, they were ministers of the faith," I explained. "Freedom fighters in a sense. They fought to earn our equality as a race and to destroy the barriers of race hate. They were mighty warriors. However, they didn't fight to give us the right to shoot, stab, rape, and kill one another."

"That's cool," a thin brother said, smiling. He was trying to dial his cell phone while talking to me.

I shook my head and asked him to put the phone away. "I want to talk to you about something. Deacon Bailey couldn't be with you today. You know he is with his wife, who is expecting another baby. But he sends his greetings to you."

Eagerly, the circle of boys and a handful of girls tightened around me, who they respected as a straight-shooting guy. Nobody had anything bad to say about me.

"First, let me say that I'm really worried about you all and our future," I said. "I think you have lost faith in yourselves. I think you have bought into that idea that you are less than human."

Some of the teens shook their heads and waved their hands in dismissal of my suggestion. Others just stared at me as if they were hearing this for the first time. But they were curious to see what I would say.

"I know the modern black church must try something new," I said. "In a sense, the church has failed you. It has failed to understand you, to reach out to you. It has failed because it has given up on true Christianity, which teaches us to be selfless, tolerant, and generous. I understand why you don't trust us."

"That's why a lot of young people don't go to church," one boy said. "The church members are so righteous and stuff. They know everything. All they preach is that we're sinners and we are going to hell. They say we're going to burn forever in that lake of fire."

I walked among them, gesturing with both hands, as if weaving a spell. "We have failed you by not telling you what you need to live in this life. We have told you to expect instant results. We did not tell you to go slow, to achieve your goals step by step. We set you guys up for failure. You, you young men and women, must stick to a plan to advance your life. Use your willpower and discipline. Have big goals but take little steps. Reward yourself for all and any progress toward your goals. Reflect on what's important to you. Take pride in yourselves. Take yourself seriously."

A teenage boy, his head in dreadlocks, stood and cut me off. "We honor you as our elders. We know about your endurance, your strength, and your struggles, but that is not going to do any good in our world. That is the past. That is history. We have to make our own way."

"And so what if we fail," another teen said sourly. "I agree with my boy. You old guys cannot live our lives for us. We got to do it for ourselves."

I stared at the group, really looking at them, this new future of my race. This was the young generation of the post-racial Negro in the era of President Barack Obama. I realized that they were in the process of becoming, in the process of discovery. But I wondered about the intentions of a merciful God and these fresh young sprouts.

We are killing ourselves, I thought as I watched them. *How can they live fuller, more loving lives? For many of these young men and women, it is not a good time to be alive.*

I motioned for the teen to sit down and scooted my chair closer to them. "Listen, we as a race, as a community, cannot do like we have done in the past. We cannot fail. There are new rules in this modern society. We have to step up and protect our community, our women, our kids, our old folks. Too much blood has been spilled already. We cannot compete unless we get an education and concentrate on things other than basketball, rap music, and sex with as many people as we can. Other communities are preparing themselves and we must do likewise. We must compete with all races and nationalities and cultures. Time is running out."

However, the group sat there, stone-faced and unmoved. They had heard this all before. It seemed that all the older folks did was talk, talk, talk. No action. That was nothing to get aroused about.

Suddenly, there was applause in the rear of the room. I turned to look in that direction and spotted a woman at the end of the rows of pews. I smiled at her.

The woman walked to the group, nodded a greeting to me, and embraced the teen with the dreadlocks. They talked among themselves and ignored the rest of the group, who started to scatter. I watched them and listened to their chatter about roughnecks, outlaws, and thugs in the hood. A few said a series of very flattering remarks about me and the consensus was that I did an adequate job filling in for Deacon Bailey.

"I'm impressed with you but you ain't me," the teen with the dreadlocks said to me. "It's hard being a young black man today. Everybody wants you to fail, even some of the people in your own community."

I shook his hand and agreed with him. I noticed he never looked me in the eyes. It was unnerving.

"Are you going to be here next week?" the teen asked me.

"I don't know," I said. "The deacon might have his business all squared away by then. We'll see."

Smiling, the woman introduced herself as Miss Collier and her son as Noah. She presented me with her business card and suggested I come around to her apartment to talk with her and her son. She hinted that it was important as her son began walking toward the exit.

I said farewell, pocketed the card, and ran out to the parking lot to rush to speak to a hastily arranged meeting of incoming freshmen at one of the community colleges. Although my schedule was almost full, I could not resist talking with young people just starting out. This was something that gave me the utmost pleasure. I never passed up an opportunity to speak with our youth.

CHAPTER 16

THE OTHER MAN

And besides this, giving all diligence, add to your faith, virtue; and to virtue knowledge.
—2 Peter 1:5

My aunt called me from the nursing home that night, saying she wanted to hear my voice and check if I was all right. She joked she had the teenage attendant sneak her in some ribs and greens, but now she was paying for it with a headache. Her laugh was like that of a kid who got away with something.

"When we love, we risk being hurt again," she advised. "When we love, we can be hurt by betrayal and disappointment. Get back out there. You've mourned enough."

"I don't know if I can," I said. "I still miss her."

Since the tragedy and the funerals, I didn't look at any suitable females or entertain any ideas of love or romance. My men friends jumped on me, arguing that such opportunities for intimacy should not be wasted. I was still in shock. Life was a constant blur, situations to be mastered, and scenes of row after row of faces. It was nearing two years and some. Although I no longer cried for my family regularly, I felt the pain and loneliness. I avoided anything to do with Cupid or affection or even desire.

"Clint, you work too hard," my aunt warned. "Everything is work for you. You have got to take it easy or you'll crack. Take some time for yourself. Don't let your prime go by, crying over spilled milk. Keeping busy is one thing but you're overdoing it."

That next day, I got a large envelope from an anonymous source. It contained a color photo of Terry at a swank club, wearing a skintight dress, showing off her lovely breasts. By the manner of dress of both men and women, it must have been an elegant and classy event. I could tell Terry was enjoying herself by the radiance of her smile and glow of her skin.

A note was paper clipped to the single photo, saying the person would call me on Friday. It said in printed letters, "We need to talk."

What event was this? Who are these people? I couldn't remember what night this was taken. The men looked like sugar daddies, dressed in well-cut Italian suits, their poses a little familiar to be just a business event. *What was Terry doing there?*

The expected call came to the church, a male's tenor voice, and was polite and courteous. Somehow he knew this number and my schedule. I wondered, *what else does he know about me? And what is this all about?* I didn't want to stir up something that was best left undisturbed.

He introduced himself as Erskine Ball, a married man who had been seeing my wife shortly before her death. I was immediately angry at him and the idea that he could invade my grief.

"Clint . . . Can I call you Clint?" He sounded very passive. "We need to talk. I'm so sorry that everything ended as it did. I want to talk to you and explain some things."

I was outraged. I called him some really vulgar names and threatened to hang up, but deep inside, I wanted to know what had happened to Terry in the final days in her life.

"Will you shut up and listen?" he said. "I know you're upset. I would be too. But I want to get some things off my chest and I think you should hear me out. There are important pieces to this puzzle that will let you sleep better at night. All I ask is that you hear me out, please."

I stared at the phone and wondered if I could learn about my wife's odd behavior from a total stranger. I said a quick, silent prayer, asking the Lord to show me what I must do.

"Clint, let me talk to you and explain some things," he pleaded. "That's all. Terry said you are a good man, a man of God, and full of understanding. Give me a few minutes. I'm trying to deal with this whole thing as well. I know you are. Maybe we can help each other."

I relented and agreed to meet him at a coffee shop on One Hundredth and Broadway on the West Side. The Metro Café. We went back and forth on the time of the meeting in the afternoon, but settled on three o'clock sharp. He politely thanked me and hung up. I sat there at the desk, wondering what I had just done.

Friday afternoon came very fast. I took a cab from the church, asking Dr. Smart for a deacon to fill in for me. He obliged me. However, I didn't tell him what I was going to do. In fact, nobody knew and that was fine with me.

At the café, I recognized him right away. He was tall, brown skinned, balding, and dressed casually in a white shirt and jeans. The rest of the people were terribly young, teens and tweens, with some over legal age. They were a noisy lot. There was the steady chatter of dishes and cups carted around by the servers.

I shook his hand firmly and looked him in the face. He pointed to the seat across from him and walked away to get me a cup of coffee. The thing that bothered me was he didn't ask me; he just assumed that I drank coffee. That action said a lot about him.

"Clint, we have much to talk about," he said when he returned, carrying two cups of coffee. "Terry was a wonderful woman, but then you know that. She was full of life. A bit quirky, a bit zany, but totally alive."

"I know that," I said, wondering where all of this was going.

He put three cubes of sugar into his black coffee and doused it with milk. "I'll start from the beginning. I met Terry at a holiday party I catered for Goldman Sachs. She was there with a friend, Marthe, who worked there in the accounting department. I noticed her standing in a circle of men listening to her raunchy jokes and watching her breasts bob up and down when she laughed."

"Was the photo you sent me? Was that taken at the party?"

"I knew Marthe from the old days in college," he said, sipping. "She took the picture. I wondered about this curvy, dark-haired woman who commanded so much attention. At first, I thought she was a little loose, but then I could see I had judged her wrong."

I was curious about him. "Erskine, what did you say that you do for a living?"

"I'm a chef at the Lulu Grill in Midtown. Fine food, good décor, and great service. You should stop in sometime. I'll set you up with a good meal."

"How did you seduce my wife?" I asked.

"Clint, I didn't seduce her. She was drinking heavily at the party, one shot after another. She'd do anything once she got drunk. But then you know that. The guys were massing around her and I yanked her out of there. It was like she was starving for affection and love. I can usually spot a gold-digger or a tramp and she wasn't neither of those types. She just wanted fun."

"Drinking always got her into trouble, Erskine."

"Terry was something else," he said, "I loved her sweet, shy smile. When I saw her, I was totally thunderstruck. I fell in lust just like a youth."

"So you didn't love her?" I finally got around to the coffee. It was lukewarm but drinkable.

"Oh yes, I loved her as much as I could," he said cheerfully. "She said it didn't matter who I was. She didn't want to know my name. It didn't matter to her that I was married. I'm old enough to realize how uncontrollable lust and physical desire can be. I also know the strange coincidences that can bring two people together."

I listened to what he had to say. This was another Terry, another woman I didn't know, another woman with her own share of secrets. "Do you think she loved you?"

"Clint, I think Terry felt like she was in jail," he replied. "She told me that nobody had ever told her she was pretty before. She told me this at the party. She sat on my lap and started wiggling, joking that I needed to learn to relax. The woman didn't like talking during sex. I didn't know what to make of her. She told me she wanted me very much. All of this happened that first night of the party. We got a room and she refused to leave before we climbed into bed one last time."

I couldn't believe this. My mother was right. She knew I had made a wrong choice of a wife.

"In the morning, Terry was already up, dressed in my white shirt and her gold panties." He smiled. "She was brushing her teeth with my toothbrush and looking at her watch. My briefcase was wide open. I don't know what she was looking for. She said she must get home and would call me later."

I was mad. "I often told her she was pretty, all of the time."

"Women love to hear they are pretty. They never get tired of hearing it. Terry craved attention. She didn't mind that I wanted to do more than kiss. She welcomed it. Her body never seemed to be satisfied. She was always aroused, just waiting and wanting."

"Erskine, where did you meet up with her?"

"Usually in hotels or motels. Sometimes we'd meet two or three times a week. She wanted to meet more."

"Did your wife suspect something?" I asked. I always wondered how these men could get away with affairs. No sense of guilt or conscience.

"No, she knew I worked late. There was always a special event or two at the restaurant and most of the workers covered for me. She didn't think anything of it, the late nights and missed calls."

His marriage sounded like mine. "How long have you been married?"

"Almost six years."

"Erskine, why did you do it?" I folded my arms across my chest.

"I don't know," he said, draining the cup. "Terry was the opposite of my wife. My wife was cool, calm, and controlled. She's from the Midwest. But Terry was like a sensual fire. We had tons of sex, in hallways, in elevators, in locked bathrooms of clubs, even in parking lots against cars. She always wanted it. Did you have sex at home?"

"Yes, we did it often," I answered. "However, I didn't think sex was a problem. I thought she was just getting neurotic."

"Did you talk to her like a man to a woman? Were you friends? Did she share anything about herself?"

"I tried, but it was difficult during the last months." I was stunned by his questioning.

"We just clicked right away," he said, watching a young girl walking suggestively across the café. "There was an honesty between us where she told me the most intimate details of her life. We shared secrets that she probably wouldn't have told anybody else, including you. I could tell she wanted to be with me. We talked about the closeness and completeness she felt toward me. She came to admire, trust, and lean on me."

"But I was her husband and father to her children." I said it aloud, in shock. I didn't know Terry after all.

"As Terry talked about you, I started to understand I was probably the first man who ever really took her serious." He sighed. "I was the first and only man who listened to her, supported her, and urged her to develop her own strength. I became her teacher, healer, mentor, and best friend."

"Why did you marry?"

He shrugged. "Because I loved my wife. There was no doubt."

"How could you mislead my wife?" I knew Terry was needy and thought she was a victim. Now I realized I was wrong about her.

He stood up and asked me if I wanted a fresh cup of coffee. I had barely touched the other cup. I nodded.

When he returned, he went on about the sordid intimacy of their relationship, almost rubbing my nose in it. "Clint, I restrained myself for as long as I could, withholding my desire in the first few weeks, wanting to assure her that she would not be hurt by me emotionally or sexually. As I said before, she knew I was married but she didn't care. We met for drinks after work and I took her in my arms and kissed her. She wanted attention, loved it. That was that. She was waiting for me to make the first move and when I did, she jumped into this hot sexual relationship without a pause. She was smoldering, ripe, and eager."

"What did she say about our family and us as a couple?"

He screwed up his face. "Terry considered your marriage as over and talked about all of the shattered love affairs she'd had. We talked long and hard about them. She wanted to know why she had them and how she could break the pattern. You were bad for her. She said you and the kids kept her from growing as a person."

"Terry had some self-destructive tendencies," I offered. "And I put up with them. She could be extremely needy and demanding. She always wanted her way."

"I know that," her ex-lover said. "But she wanted to change. She wanted us to be a permanent item so we could have a healthy, stable relationship. She wanted me to leave my wife and be with her. I was tired of sneaking around on my wife. I stopped seeing Terry for a while."

"What did she do?" I realized this was the frantic period before she began acting strange.

He stared at the door leading to the Broadway exit. "Either women give too little of themselves or give too much. In time, everything got out of sync. I wanted out. I saw the real woman in her. I needed time to think."

"Terry wanted the real thing, a lasting relationship," I said, drinking my fresh cup of java. "But how could you do that when you were married to another woman? Somebody had to get hurt either way."

"And that somebody had to be Terry." He looked sad.

"You crushed her. You destroyed her emotionally."

"I remember one of the last times we talked like civilized human beings, just before I went on the cruise with my wife," he recalled. "I called her and told her I made a serious mistake and we should stop seeing each other. She freaked out. She cussed me out. I said I wanted to save my marriage. Also, she was getting obsessive, nutty, and I didn't know what she would do. After work, she stalked my every move and followed my wife in the daytime. I was afraid she would hurt my wife."

"Terry felt rejected and totally manic," I said to him. "Your breakup left her completely unbalanced. We suffered in my home from your stupidity. Didn't you know how fragile she was?"

"Not really." He said it, then paused while collecting his thoughts.

I couldn't believe that. He must have known how she was unraveling.

"I didn't realize how serious the whole thing had become," he continued in a quiet voice. "We met outside my job one night. She immediately threatened my wife, saying she'd kill her. Or hire somebody to do it. My wife was the barrier to our happiness. It was crazy. She said I must become a part of her life. I shook my head no. Then she hit me, attacked me right in front of my job. No woman had ever done that before. She was like a madwoman, totally in a rage, hit me and kept hitting me until I held her arms behind her back."

"What did you do after that?"

He closed his eyes and took a deep breath. "Boy, was I scared. I didn't know what she was capable of doing. I pushed her in a cab and we continued struggling. I wanted to get her away from my workplace. She pounded me real good. My head was numb. Blood was coming from my nose and mouth. I let her out two

blocks from your house and stopped at a fast food joint
and cleaned up."

"Did you get in contact with her after your attack?"

"She called me at my job and harassed me," he said.
"She called me at home all times of night and would
hang up. My wife wanted to get the phone company to
trace the calls but I told her that it must be some kids.
Pranks. I was still worried about Terry. We went on the
cruise and I told Terry afterward that it was definitely
over. I told my wife about the affair during the cruise
and she said she already knew. She was happy that I
had come to my senses."

"You didn't know that Terry killed herself and the
kids?" I wanted to hold him responsible for their murders. I wanted to label him a killer.

"Not until I saw the newspapers and the TV," he
murmured and put his head down on his arms. He was
crying. "I'm sorry, so sorry. I didn't mean it to end like
this. I was such a fool."

I drank my coffee, watched her former lover for a
few minutes. He didn't stir. He kept on crying. I had
worked through much of my grief and pain, and I
needed to make plans for the future and change the
course of my life. The past was at my back. For once, I
was putting together a picture of what kind of woman,
wife, and mother Terry really was and I didn't like it
one bit. I hated that we were complete strangers. We
just lived together under one roof, had two kids in common, and were bonded by a false marriage vow. It was
all a lie, a big lie.

CHAPTER 17

JUST ONE MORE CHANCE

Fight the good fight of the faith, take hold of the eternal life to which you were called.
                                        —1 Timothy 6:12

The telephone call came late one night. It was the panicked voice of Miss Collier, on the verge of hysteria and desperation, asking me to come over this instant. Noah was in trouble, deep trouble, with the law.

"You gotta be kiddin'." I put down the phone, muttering about nobody in a sane mind would call this late. I was in my pajamas. I promised I would come over, probably needed to take a cab because I was parked on the right side of the street. I didn't want to risk losing my parking space.

Once at the elegant apartments of The Madison Terraces, the doorman halted me and announced my arrival. The doorman told me that three policemen visited Miss Collier about two hours before and her son was being held at the local precinct. Waving toward a bank of elevators, he pointed me in that direction, noting how well dressed I was at this time of night.

I walked down the hall and stopped in front of the door. Before I could ring the bell, the door was yanked open and Miss Collier fell into my arms, with a tearstained face and an embrace that was very unlady-like.

"He's been arrested," she wept, still clutching me. "They said he was a part of a gang who robbed lockers at health clubs, busting locks and taking cash and other valuables. The thefts took place while the victims worked out and the gang had a lookout who would make sure that nobody caught them."

"Who are 'they'?" I asked.

"The police," she replied. "They called me at work. I tried to get you but you were out. I know you are busy but I thought you would like to know. The police said he and this gang had been stealing right through the holidays, Thanksgiving and Christmas. The chief detective said they had a task force that specialized in these robberies but they had never caught anybody until now. The police collared Noah and three guys. All of them had police records but him."

"What do you want me to do?" I'd just taken over the sessions at the church a few months ago, but I liked the boy.

"I really don't know," she said. "Just talk to him. He'll listen to you. He trusts you. He talks about you like you are a relative."

"How did he get mixed up with this bunch of thieves?"

The woman pulled me into the living room to sit me down on the sofa. "I don't know. He started hanging with these people after school. The gang bought day passes and used them to case the locker rooms. Noah and the others dressed like the people who attended the gyms for workouts. The police were alerted when some of the gangs used stolen credit cards to buy the passes at the gyms."

"Noah seems like he is closed emotionally, shut off from himself," I said sadly. "He never looks you right in the eyes. He looks at the floor. I don't think he thinks a lot of himself. What happened to him?"

"Life failed him," answered Miss Collier, sitting in a plush chair opposite me. "His father should have stayed with us. He left us because I was cheating. I had this very real need to get close to men. His father should have stayed."

"Did the cops find anything of value on him?" I asked, changing the subject.

"The police found some cash on him," she said. "He didn't even try to hide it. It was almost as if he was proud of being a thief. He doesn't think sometimes. Often he's like a kid, never having grown up."

"That's not good."

"I know it isn't," she said, folding her arms.

"How much is bail?" I asked. "Is it his first offense?"

Miss Collier rose and asked me if I wanted anything to drink. "Yes, this is his first time doing something like this," she replied. "Three months ago I wouldn't have suspected he was doing something like this. He was a normal teenager. He was a regular son. He did everything I told him."

"Why do you think he did this mess?"

She went into the kitchen, adding a little wiggle in her ample hips. There, she began rummaging around in the cupboards, looking for something. She knelt down and searched in the cabinet behind things. Afterward, she stood still, permitting her mind to think; then she walked over to the refrigerator and felt around on top of it.

"I knew I put the wine there," she said. "I just knew it."

But I refused the wine. I didn't need any alcohol.

"My father warned me about Noah," she said. "He said my child is having temper tantrums, and that was a sign that something else was wrong. When he went to grade school, he hurt the other children. Now, he has changed. My uncle says it is the result of puberty. I don't know what to believe. Seventeen years old. Noah is at the place where he is not quite a man and still very much a boy. Puberty for a boy is a very scary time. Is that true?"

"May I?" I asked, placing a pack of cigarettes on the table. "I know some people don't like the cigarette smoke."

Miss Collier finally really looked at me. A total once-over. I was stout, but physically fit. Kinda tall. My eyes were sad and gentle for a man who had seen so much of life.

"Yes, please do," she remarked. "Do you have another one?'

We smoked our cigarettes in silence, but the idea of coming up with something grownup and positive was getting in the way. *What can be done about Noah? How can he keep out of trouble? What rewards would he honor if he remains out of the grasp of the law? Some money, fine clothing, nice jewelry, or a car. But used.*

"Is there any male figure in Noah's life?" I asked her.

The woman drank some of the wine and coughed. "At present, there are none, nobody, no men," she said. "I was trying to be a cougar. Like on the *Oprah* show. She had some older women who were dating young men. I tried to do that but they kept me out all night. Noah would see me a little tipsy and crawling in here all times of night. Boys are very impressionable. I didn't know that. I started drinking after my marriage went on the rocks. He didn't like the men I dated."

"Why?" I stretched out my legs.

"I was with a guy just a little older than Noah and we were getting intimate," she said, smiling smugly. "Nothing really nasty. Just some necking and heavy petting. I was fully clothed. Noah came into my room and pointed my gun to his head. He threatened my lover, scared the heck out of him. Excuse my French. Since then, he has been my constant protector. No more men."

"You should have called the cops on him after he did a stunt like that. Somebody might have gotten hurt. Anything could have happened. Why did Noah react so strongly to this man?"

She filled her mouth with wine. I didn't say anything.

"What was this fella's name?" I asked.

"Buddy. I was very loyal to him," she said. "I waited for him. My ex used to say I had no patience. But I waited for Buddy to do the bid for robbery and assault. He was at a prison upstate. Whenever I visited him during his stretch, he didn't mind me looking haggard. I knew when he got out that the good times would follow. He knew I liked to dance and party, club hopping, but he trusted me. I waited for him because I knew nobody could do for me what he did."

"And what was that, Miss Collier?"

She grinned widely. "Rough sex. He knew I liked rough sex."

"I see, but something has really hurt Noah deeply," I said. "Have you ever asked what happened? There is a reason why he's acting out this way. Basically, Noah is a good boy. I know that."

She took a lungful of cigarette smoke and exhaled. "My husband, his father leaving did a number on his head. Carl, his father, and I were happy for a while, had sex every night. In time, he could sense me getting restless sexually. Then I started cheating on him."

I leaned back in the chair, frowned. "Not too graphic, please."

"Gradually it became an open marriage, doing whatever we wanted," she admitted. "I did something I wanted to do and that was to go to bed with a woman. It was nice but I discovered I wasn't bisexual. Being together and apart created problems, emotional problems. It was difficult and complicated."

"Why didn't you just walk away?" I quizzed her.

"Because I loved Noah's father," she said, twisting the cigarette around on the ashtray. "Sex is a great thing but not everybody gets to fall in love. We didn't have to creep around. We had to practice safe sex. No surprises. We both took each other for granted. That's deadly for a marriage."

"That's true," I said.

"Reverend, do you ever miss the sex?" she asked.

I picked up the discarded cigarette butt and relit it. "Oh yes, I miss Terry in every way. We had a few moments where we fought and said horrible things to each other but I knew everything would work out. I remember one time she fell in love with this friend of her mother's and I thought she was going to leave me for him."

"Did she love him?"

"Yes, she did. She said he made her tremble."

She grinned as if she knew the feeling well. "Do you think she would have left you? And the kids as well?"

I blew the smoke out through my parted lips. "I knew Terry could love men without ever thinking of leaving me. She was a good mother, at least in the beginning. She became confused toward the end."

She saw the pain in my hooded eyes and knew to back off.

"So what are you going to do about Noah?" I asked her directly. I really didn't want to get sidetracked.

"I don't know what to do," she said softly. "I've done everything I can to help him. I'm almost played out."

I knew what they needed. I knew something about answered prayers, steadfast faith, the powerful union of souls, our lives in partnership with the Lord. But I couldn't explain that to her. I knew that she had endured a long silence from the Almighty and what she needed was a bit of comfort and solace from her crisis.

"What are you not telling me?" I questioned her.

"For a while, Noah has not been acting like himself," Miss Collier said. "He's real irritable. He is very uncommunicative and not responsive to anything I do. His energy is erratic. Totally manic. Sometimes he gets real hyper from exhaustion. He goes and goes and goes until he passes out."

"Do you think he's depressed?"

She reached for the pack of cigarettes and lit another one. She said, "If you asked him, he would never admit that he was depressed.

"And Noah has never talked back to me, never." She bristled. "He's come awfully close to disrespecting me but he would never do it. I know I'm probably worrying too much but something is not right. I know there are no easy remedies. Often he just stares at me like I did him wrong. I want the best for him. I know he can do better. Is it wrong for me to demand that he be the best? He's not one of these roughnecks in the streets. I don't know what to do. One of my aunts said I should get his father to come back home, just for the sake of the kid."

"Don't do that unless you have really thought it out," I warned.

The telephone rang in the kitchen and she walked in the room and answered it. All I could see of her was her gesturing her arms with her back to me. Her voice was loud and high-pitched. She was pleading to her caller for mercy and money and time to get her son out of jail.

She cursed a string of rude words in a shriek as she slammed the receiver down.

"What's wrong, Miss Collier?"

She stood with her arms folded, breathing heavily, and said: "A lawyer friend went down there and he said Noah is having a hard time. The other inmates are picking on him because he is so young. He said I got to get him out of there."

I left but not before saying a long prayer for Noah's protection and freedom. I touched her on the shoulder softly and smiled. With her face upturned, it was as though she wanted me to kiss her, but the moment passed and I walked into the hall.

It was the next morning. I turned over on the bed and covered my ears. A blast of city sounds rushed me with a vengeance. I walked to the bathroom and relieved myself. After washing my hands, I moved to the kitchen, emptied the coffee filter and replaced it. I wanted a good cup of java so I poured fresh water into the pot.

I looked between the blinds and saw it had rained the previous night. Silent deluge. Everything was wet.

That was when the cell phone rang. I picked it up and saw that I didn't recognize the number. The voice of the young teen was very calm, flat, and disconnected. Something was wrong with its tone.

"Reverend, I am out," Noah announced. "Free as a bird."

"Who got you out?" I asked him.

"A friend." The teen giggled.

"Where are you?" I asked. "Does your mother know where you are? She is very worried about you. She was trying to get your bail money all through the night."

He scoffed. "She doesn't know where I am. Nobody does."

"Don't you think you should go home?"

"No," Noah shot back. "Why should I do that?"

"I advise you to check in at least, so she won't have to worry," I suggested. "You don't want your mother to worry unnecessarily."

He barked angrily. "She doesn't care."

"That is your mother. You know you only get one. And that's it."

Noah coughed harshly like he was clearing something deep down in his lungs. "Do you know anything about getting high? I'm going to do a lot of getting high now that I'm out of jail. Screw that good boy stuff. I'm going to raise hell."

"What you need to do is to sit somewhere and think about what you did to get you in jail," I said. "That's what you need to do. Look over what you have been doing lately."

"Why?" Noah's voice went up an octave.

"Because you don't want to repeat your performance by going back to jail," I said. "Did you get enough of that? Jail is no joke."

"I know that." He was somber.

"Can you call your mother?" I asked. "Do you want me to call her? I will if you want me to do it."

"I'll get around to it," Noah said bitterly. "I'm feeling too good to get lectured over and over. I need to cool out. My mother brings me down. All she does is to make me feel like a failure. I hate that feeling."

"Are you high?"

"Pills, Reverend," he replied, slightly out of it. "Pills to bring me down. Pills to lift me up. Pills to take me out of myself. Pills to chase the bad feelings away."

"If you get high, they will take you back to jail," I said.

He coughed again, this time much worse. "Reverend, I took pills before I started to drink or smoke. I remember when Dad was there in the house and I couldn't get up or dressed or go to school. And I couldn't sleep either. My mother always had something in her medicine cabinet. She had Valium or Lithium or something like that. Oh man, I'd get messed up."

I heard car horns, the roar of a passing bus, and people walking back and forth, talking and laughing. I wished I knew where Noah was. The teen kept talking and talking and talking.

"After Dad left, I really started to mess up in school and on the streets," Noah said with a chuckle. "My mother knew something was going on but she didn't know what. I looked like a bag of bones. I lost a lot of weight. I used to pass out, right at the dinner table. Zonked. Sometimes I stayed in the bed all day."

"And you don't think that something is wrong with you?"

He laughed sourly. "I told my mother I wanted to die. This life is just not worth it. Once I wanted this girl at my high school to go ahead and cut my throat. But she wouldn't do it. I begged and pleaded with her. No dice."

"Go to your mother," I asked. "Call her, please."

"Just before I got into all this trouble, I started seeing things where they were not there," he said. "Seeing things in my sleep and while I was awake. One time a large, long black snake appeared on the sheet, just materialized right before my eyes, and crawled toward me. I need a little buzz."

"Tell me where you are and I'll come to you," I suggested. "Just tell me. I'll be there in a jiffy."

"Nobody cares about me," Noah whined. "They would be better off without me. I'm just taking up space on this earth."

"Wait a darn minute," I said. "Don't you quit on life. Don't give up."

"I don't care if I die." The teen sighed. "This is much more than I can bear. It's crashing down on me and I cannot get out of its way."

"Call your mother," I said. "Let me come there to you. You're not alone. I am here with you. Your mother is here with you. God is with you. You can make it through this hard time."

"I went to jail," the teen cried. "I brought disgrace and shame on my family. My mother cannot walk in the city without looking down. Nobody wants me around. I'm bad news."

"Please call her, please, please."

"Screw you and my mother," he yelled and hung up.

At the rectory that night, Dr. Smart entered my office, wearing a very long face. I was already there with Mother Ford and Deacon Hines talking about the vandalism done to the neon sign in front of the church. He greeted everybody and began talking in a quiet voice.

"God bless us, death will come to us someday, to us all," Dr. Smart said, sounding like a country parson. "Noah's mother just called me and said she found the boy on the bathroom floor with a gunshot wound in the face."

We gasped. It hit me especially hard, since I talked with the teen just hours ago. I knew he was troubled and on the verge of a breakdown.

"Noah's mother said he let himself in while she was out," Dr. Smart added. "His body was covered with plenty of cuts and bruises, indicating signs of a violent struggle. That probably happened in jail. Knuckle scrapes. Deep purple bruises on his wrists where he had been tightly held. Cut lips, bloody ears, and three teeth missing."

"Oh my Lord," Mother Ford mumbled softly.

"Noah's mother said he hugged the old Dominican woman across the hall and told her how he was sorry and cried," Dr. Smart continued. "I guess that was when he went into the apartment and did the deed. I can't believe he would kill himself. I will never understand young people killing themselves."

Deacon Hines, always a practical man, wanted to know about the weapon. The death gun. "Where did he get the gun to shoot himself with?"

"I don't know, Deacon," Dr. Smart remarked.

For some reason, I kept silent with the terrible knowledge that Noah's mother kept a gun in the house. She said it was for their protection.

Deacon Hines shook his head. "It's too easy to get a gun. Anybody can get one and nothing good happens when you get your hands on a gun. I knew this boy. I thought he was too levelheaded to do something like that."

"A lot of young black boys are killing themselves," Dr. Smart said sadly. "They just give up. They think they are not wanted by this world. Truthfully, the world doesn't care about them."

"We should have helped him," Deacon Hines replied. "He was out there by himself and nobody cared if he lived or died."

I took offense to that remark. "I cared and his mother cared. He was not alone. He just thought he was alone."

Dr. Smart exhaled deeply. "There's no telling what goes on in somebody's mind. A person can appear so normal and then do something like this. I don't think anybody could have helped him."

"Did he leave a note?" I asked.

"Yes, he did," the older minister answered. "It said in cut-out newspaper letters: I Know My Rights."

CHAPTER 18

RIGHT FROM THE BEGINNING

Let us hold unswervingly to the hope we pro-
fess, for He who promised is faithful.
                                        —Hebrews 10:23

The sky was gray and flat. I was trying to calm myself down. I was angry at myself. I couldn't bring myself to walk back with the others from the graveside. I had never done that before. I stayed at the grave and asked the Holy Spirit to forgive me for not watching over Noah more closely. I didn't pay enough attention to him.

Did I do that to Terry? Not pay enough attention to her? Neglect and abandon her when she needed me most? I know I tried very hard in both instances, with Terry and Noah. Sometimes trying is not enough.

"Miss Collier, can . . . Can . . . ?" I moved through the people toward the sorrowful woman. I reached for her. She immediately stiffened and pulled away.

The hearse pulled up. Miss Collier waved me into the car and waited for me to enter it. There was an old woman and a small boy sitting there on the rear seat. I scooted up and across from them. Later, I learned the old woman was a trusted friend of Miss Collier's mother, accompanied by the child on loan from her sister's daughter. They flashed me their timid, weak smiles and went on staring out the window.

"I'm glad you decided to go with us," Miss Collier said.

"I was looking for you after the funeral," I said. "It's funny that people always want to see the parents break down and collapse in grief. They don't know that you are in such pain. It's no joke."

She hid her eyes with her hands and turned to the window. "Noah quit on life. He quit. He quit on me . . . on me . . . on me. I'm his mother. He was weak, emotionally and spiritually weak."

A cold pause hung in the hearse.

"Do you miss your kids?" Miss Collier then asked me.

I looked up and saw the old woman's face was frowning at her question. She clucked her tongue against her teeth. "Don't ask him that," she said to Miss Collier.

"I miss them badly and my wife," I assured her.

The old woman mumbled something under her breath that we couldn't hear. It was a bad question. If that same question were asked of me earlier, I would have come apart and started sobbing all over the place.

"Most reverends are too controlling, too self-involved," Miss Collier said. "Are you like that? What gets under your skin, Reverend?"

I smiled. "I have to confess, my work comes first."

"Do you lie, like most men?"

"No, I try not to."

"Did you cheat on your wife before she died?"

I leered at her. "Never."

"Carl, my ex, said to me I shouldn't worry because Noah'd grow out of his rebellion," Miss Collier said sadly, abruptly changing the topic. "He told me don't worry about my son. It was a boy thang. He also told me that all young black kids, males, go through this surly stage. This hood attitude. I don't accept that. Noah was sick. Sick in body and soul. Carl didn't know what he was talking about."

"Lord bless my Noah," the old woman said. She took a deep breath, for nothing could bring back what was lost.

Miss Collier shut her eyes as if to blot the old woman's voice from her mind and began mouthing words. "'Our greatest eloquence, the pith of the joy and sorrow in our unbreakable hearts, comes when we lift up our faces and talk to God, person to person. Ours is the truest dignity of Man, the dignity of the undefeated.'"

"Who wrote that?" I asked.

"The show business performer Ethel Waters wrote this in 1951," she remarked proudly. "It's from a book that I stole from my grandmother. She had this passage underlined."

"Very beautiful," I said.

"I nearly forgot how to breathe," said the old woman, who wet her lips with her tongue and dramatically spat out the bitter taste of sorrow. "It was a lovely service, very lovely."

"Being a teacher, you remember all kinds of trivia and useless junk," Miss Collier laughed. "Just like one of those fans recalls all of those stats and meaningless facts about their sports and the players. Utterly meaningless."

I grinned. The old woman sat very quietly, holding the little boy. I smiled at the warmth of her love, looked around, and settled back down. I thought of my lost little boy, my son, and my quirky girl too. Terry took that from me. *How can I forgive her? How?*

Maybe I never saw her for what she was, I thought as I watched the boy. *I should have seen the red flags and the other warning signs. A real man would have seen those things. A real man. I cannot say that I was a real man, because I would have satisfied Terry at her heart level. If I had done that, she would not have*

*strayed. There was something that led her to believe
that our love was a painful ball and chain.*

The old woman was staring at me and that stare did
not relent. I started to say something but I let the moment pass. It was my attempt to reconcile good and
evil. And I felt like I was not doing the job. His Lord's
divine work. I was fumbling, tripping up the stairs, and
letting things fall between the cracks.

My family was what mattered to me, I continued
thinking. *I knew I was not perfect. I was working out
the kinks before all of this mess happened. I wanted to
prove my love. When we were in sync, we had it made.
We were peaceful, easy with each other, as tight as
ticks. Heart and soul. Some friends said it was hard to
tell when she ended and I began. She opened her heart
and knew I would not break it. That glow was inside
us. Like young lovers spooning around each other. We
as one. So full was my life.*

"We're all getting up there in years," the old woman
said. "All of us getting old and rushing toward death.
God just took him before his time."

"He wanted to die and he told me so," Miss Collier
said. "Why would somebody want to kill himself? He
was too young. He had not lived yet."

The little boy lifted his head and listened. He seemed
to understand everything the grownups said, but
maybe not the nuances of their remarks.

"I don't think you could have solved Noah's problems," the old woman said to me. "Something was
gnawing at his soul. Mammon was in him."

Miss Collier perked up. "Noah wanted to live, too.
Even though he wanted to die, be dead, he wanted to
live in the worst way. I tried to strengthen the part of
him that wanted to live. Thrive and succeed. He quit
on life."

"Noah was all bottled up," I noted. "He was afraid to reach out for help. A lot of our black boys are like that. Only at the end, there was an attempt to cry for help but it was too late. I never figured he would kill himself. "

"He could be real quiet," Noah's mother said. "He was an old soul. It was like he had been here before."

"Noah told me the other day about the night you were robbed and nearly killed," I said. "That nearly traumatized him. He wanted to be the man in the house but he felt he couldn't protect you, his mother."

"That was awhile ago," Miss Collier replied. "I was coming home from night school. I'm taking a short class at the college to shore up my resume. I was with a colleague. A white guy. These thugs, black kids, come rushing up to us, pull guns on us, and make us lie down on the street. It was insulting. It was humiliating. They robbed us of our money and jewelry."

"Did they do anything else?"

"No, thank God," she exclaimed.

I shook my head. I prayed for the forgiveness of the robbers and the strength of Miss Collier. The virus of this grief was not dead. It had us talking about things we would rather not say. I was thinking of Terry and the kids, dead and buried.

My thoughts tugged at my soul. *Maybe my wife was right when she said I was selfish, that I liked coming and going as I please. Maybe she was right when she said I didn't want to be anybody. Maybe I want the life I have now. I am not a dog. I am not a bad man. I loved Terry and the kids and I make no apologies for that.*

"How far, driver?" the old woman asked.

"We're on Broadway and soon we will turn on Seventy-ninth Street," the driver answered. "You don't mind if we use some shortcuts, Miss Collier?"

"I don't care whether you use shortcuts or not," she snapped, frowning at the people on the streets. "I blame Carl for all of this. He killed Noah. He was an alley cat. Carl would get me all heated up and then he would do his usual tricks. He'd satisfy himself, come and roll over, and fall asleep. If I wanted more, he'd get mad at me and curse. His ego got in the way."

"Some men are like that," I said. I didn't want to preach to her, not on this most solemn day.

The old woman put her finger up to her lips. "Enough of that kind of talk."

"Carl was so selfish." The grieving mother bristled. "He never thought about what I needed from our sex life. I needed love and affection, not carnal tricks."

"But you stuck it out," I added. "You didn't have to do that. You're not like anybody else. You also took good care of Noah."

Miss Collier glared at the old woman and then at the back of the driver's head. "I feel like a failure. I failed at being a parent, at being a mother. I didn't have any easy answers for Noah. He was a lost boy. I couldn't offer him any better option than killing himself."

"You don't know that." I looked at her shaking hands.

They became quiet after I said that. The old woman's aged fingers worked the boy's hair until he went to sleep. Miss Collier stared past the woman to the moving scenery and pondered about the reason of grief.

Looking at Miss Collier, I knew exactly what she was thinking, because I had been in her shoes with the loss of my loved ones. Fear and grief. *I've been totally honest with myself sometimes. I look in the mirror and frighten myself with the man I've become. I am tired and scared. I want to be a better man, not just a good man, but I fall short. Nothing was important to me but my wants, so that's what Terry thought. But that was not true. My family and my marriage were important. It was more than just two people living with each other under a roof. We shared a life together with the kids, so what happened?*

Forgive her. Forgive her so I can forgive myself. Forget and forgive. I want to be better. I will keep my mind and heart focused on the right things. The Church is my life. God is my life. I must put my soul in His work. I have more time to think about how I want to live my life starting this moment forward. Embrace His grace.

"Something like this happens, it jars you, throws you off balance, and takes your peace of mind away," Miss Collier said. "It cuts deep. Both of us have lost everything, everything in this world."

"There is no happy ending except through the Lord," I said. "Just keep moving when you want to stand still. Keep moving. Be a fighter. Be a survivor. That's what I do. I try to move through my grief. If I didn't, it would swallow me and I'd be no good to anybody, including myself."

"Can you drop me off with this child?" the old woman asked. "Cheryl, this child's mama will be there before you know it. I want to be there when she comes. Is that a trouble?"

Miss Collier shook her head no.

I looked deep into Miss Collier's sad eyes again. "We must remember that God is on our side," I said solemnly. "God cries with us when we are in pain. God wants to understand that pain and suffering. God wants us to know it is not a punishment. Our pain is a blessing. Our pain can have no meaning until we choose to know it, until we choose to own it."

Miss Collier wiped away the tears from the end of her chin. "But this really hurts. Ask any mother and she would tell you."

"I know the pain," I agreed. She had some really hard nights ahead of her.

When the hearse pulled up to the house of the old woman, Miss Collier got out as well. I looked at my watch again. As I scooted over to the window, she held the door open and pecked me on the cheek.

I grinned briefly. I felt their eyes focus on me and pulled out a cigarette. I reached over, motioned her to me again, and kissed her on the forehead. All very chaste. Now she smiled, only broader.

Once at home, I immediately knelt and repeated my new mantra. "My faith is powerful and strong. My love of God is powerful and strong, and the saved life increases my faith each minute of every day."

I knew the Lord could change my heart. My faith would get me through these hard and difficult times, for my head would remain bowed until I completed my journey. I was progressing spiritually. There was a gentle softening of my soul. Terry once called me "Mr. Band-Aid" because I was all giving to others, mending the souls of others, but when I came to her, there was nothing left. That was what she said.

On the other hand, Miss Collier didn't think of herself as a sinner. She wanted to get Noah's body into the ground quickly so she could get on with her life. She had given up on him a long time ago, but she also shouldered a part of the blame. There was no autopsy. She refused to permit it. Her church family and co-workers chipped in money toward the expenses of the funeral, the mortician, the top-of-the-line gold coffin, and the guests and the mourners.

No sooner than I removed my tie did the phone ring. It was Dr. Smart. He seemed pleased with his young protégé, hailing that I was fulfilling my divine purpose. Also, my mentor said I was not getting myself into harm, choosing not to repeat past choices and mistakes. He was proud of me.

"It's really not that bad," Dr. Smart said, thinking about his young pastor's waning grief. "Just don't blame yourself about Terry and the kids. You must ask yourself: can destiny be altered? Can you change something you know is coming? Only God can do that."

"I know that," I agreed.

Dr. Smart was very laidback. "I appreciate your purchase of the flowers for the funeral. You think of everything. You're a very thoughtful man. Now we just have to heal your heart. We have to find new ways of healing so you can deal with the challenges of the past and spark some hope for the future."

"Thank you, sir." I was pleased that I had done so well.

"I hear a click on your phone," the senior pastor said. "Is there somebody trying to get you? You should see who it is."

I switched over to the other line and heard the wailing noise of the grieving parent, Miss Collier. She was nearly hysterical.

"We need to talk, Reverend," Miss Collier said. "Can I see you? I've got a car waiting downstairs at your place. I need to see you soon."

Suddenly, I was very hot, temperature-wise, possibly from the tension of the situation. I knew what she expected of me. The perspiration ran down my face and collected at my collar. Quieting myself before my exit, I smoked a cigarette and took slow, calming breaths.

The drive over there was long and nervy. I was sent up to her apartment. When she opened the door, all the lights were out but I could see Miss Collier was visibly exhausted. There were bags under her eyes and deep creases around her mouth that I had not seen before.

She threw her arms around my neck and made me press hard against her. In the end, I hugged her back and then the scalding tears came from her bloodshot eyes. There was no reason to measure the full weight of her sorrow because her body shook like a trembling autumn leaf about to tumble to the hard ground.

CHAPTER 19

SACRIFICE

"Having been justified by faith, we have peace with God through our Lord Jesus Christ."
— Romans 5:1–2

Two days later after the funeral, a large, heavy-set woman was parked across the street from the church. She was waiting for something. Her eyes kept roaming toward the front door of the building as if she were going to ambush the next person she saw. It was snowing again. When I arrived, one of the workmen pointed the woman in the car out to me.

I got a cup of coffee and took it to my office. The large woman was now right behind me, dogging my footsteps. She tapped me on the shoulder to turn me around.

"Yes, ma'am," I said. "What can I do for you?"

"I need your help, Reverend," the woman said. "I'm Mrs. Gertrude Townsend. I belong to another church but everybody says you're like a miracle worker in this part of town. Everybody recommended you to me for this sort of a problem."

"What sort of a problem is it?" I asked.

"Can I sit down to rest my legs some?" Mrs. Townsend said. "I've got sugar and my legs swell up on me some. I cannot stay on my feet long."

We went to my office and camped there, discussing her problem. I was grumpy this day, slightly out of character, but I never let her see my displeasure.

"It's my niece, Trina," she said. "She has gone and got herself into trouble. Nobody knows that she is in a family way but me. She is very scared. She doesn't know what to do. The boyfriend is trying to pressure her to get rid of it."

"Do you know this boy?"

Mrs. Townsend sagged back into the soft comfort of the sofa and crossed her ankles. "No, I don't. The first I heard about the situation was yesterday. She called me up crying and said she wanted to come over."

"Can you talk to her parents?" I asked.

"Not really, they're old fashioned," the woman replied. "They think butter don't melt in her mouth. She used to be a good girl but she started hanging out with a bad element. She has lost interest in everything, school, grades, sports, the debate team, everything."

"What is it that you want me to do?" I quizzed her.

"Talk to her. Talk some sense into her. She'll probably listen to you. They say you work wonders with the young people around here. They respect you. She is considering an abortion and that will sure wreck her. I know it will."

I thought back to the failure of Noah, how he cried for help and support, how he was going down slow, and how I let the boy's hand slip and everything after that. Noah died because of me.

"I know firsthand about abortion," Mrs. Townsend told him. "I had one once. The quack messed me up so bad that I had bleeding problems for months on end. Then the regular doctor discovered that something was wrong with my tubes and a nasty infection had set in and I couldn't have any babies. I don't want her to go through that."

"No, I don't either."

"Are you pro-life? Most Christians are."

"I will talk to her and see what I can do." I dodged the question. I didn't like to be pigeonholed or labeled.

"You don't believe in Planned Parenthood and all that rot, do you?" she asked. "All that liberal mess."

"I believe in the Bible," I answered. "I believe in the Holy Word and try to practice what the Good Book says."

"Can I send her around to you?"

I smiled and stood up, extending my hand. "Sure. Tomorrow afternoon. About two. I'll have some time before I go back to work."

"Work?" Mrs. Townsend wondered aloud.

"Consulting and advising," I replied. I shook her hand and walked her out to the street. This was a tricky situation, anything about sex and babies, but my reputation was a good one. We made small talk on the way to the car: weather, the governor and his floozy, the holiday sales, Tiger Woods, and the congress and its absurd fight with the first black president.

Walking back to the church, I stopped to say hello to a group of elderly ladies on their way to the mall. They were smart to go in numbers, in a pack, especially after the holidays.

The following day came and two young people entered the office. The solidly built teenage boy, with his hat turned sideways, sauntered through the doorway, with his baggy jeans halfway down his butt. He was fingering a Newport behind his ear. The girl, well endowed, wore a sweater and a midrange dress that showed off some shapely legs.

"You the Holy Joe?" the boy asked. "They sent us to see you."

The girl looked around my office, taking everything into her consciousness, as if she would be forced to take a quiz on the room's contents. She seemed fidgety, very nervous, while her male companion took center stage.

"Yes, I'm the man Mrs. Townsend asked you to see," I said. "She said you guys have a problem that maybe I can help you with."

"It's her problem, not mine." The boy sniffed. "I'm not the baby's daddy. I'm allergic to reverends, deacons, and all this holy mess."

"I'm Trina, and, yeah, I got a problem," she said defiantly. "Damn, I've never missed my period before. I would spot before but it always came. To be honest, I didn't think I could have a kid. Dudes have come in me before but I never got pregnant."

"How old are you, Trina?" I asked.

"Fifteen and a half," she said, her left eye twitching. "I was afraid to tell him. I was very scared. Dudes find out you pregnant and they head for the hills. I didn't want to be alone through all this stuff."

The boy stroked her arm lovingly. "You ain't alone. I got your back."

"Reverend, you can't imagine the stress I'm under. I don't know what to do. He says he'll marry me although the baby might not be his, he says he'll work two or three jobs to support us if he has to. I only know having a baby will ruin my life."

The boy had his hands casually in his pants pockets. "Trina, she's one fine hottie. Tarik beat me to her. When I got a look at her and her slamming body, I was hooked. Some niggas spoil everything."

"Who's Tarik?"

"Tarik is my man," Trina replied. "We did another test and it came up positive. I haven't seen him since. He calls me all the time. I brought up the idea of having

an abortion because I don't think I could be responsible for another human being. He called me a freaking
baby killer."

"Abortion is serious business," I said.

"I know it is," she said. "Once it's done, it's done."

"But if you had to go through it, I would be right
there by your side," the boy said. "You know I would
not leave your side. Like I said, I got this. I got your
back."

Trina sighed and stared at the picture of a black Christ
on the cross, blood coming down on his forehead from a
crown of thorns. "Believe me, I didn't know if I wanted
to have him in my life forever. If I had the baby, he would
be right there. Tarik's good for sex but that's about all. I
can't see him in my life for the rest of my days. I'm out-
growing him already."

"How many boys did you sleep with?"

"I slept around." She laughed. "It's a pretty crazy
time in my life. I was catching it at home, especially
from my moms. I couldn't find a long-term relationship so I started sampling the crop."

"So you really don't know who the father of this baby
is?"

"Yep, it could be anybody's baby. And just think: I
used to tell my moms that I would never have kids.
When I get high, my inner slut comes out and I just
want to sex somebody."

"And abstinence . . ."

She burst out laughing. "I didn't have a steady dude.
I hung out with a lot of niggas, most of them thugs and
roughnecks. Hung out and let them do me. Most of
them guys are like dogs in heat. They will sex anything,
even each other."

"Tell him about the time Tarik gave you the STD,"
the boy yelled.

"But I don't know if it was him. It could have been one of the other niggas I was screwing with. Plus the clinic cleared it up real fast. It wasn't a big thing. I'm not going to lose sleep over this."

"This is some serious stuff," I said. "There's a life involved."

Trina saw the ashtray and reached over to her male friend and took his Newport. He lit it for her, being chivalrous. I enjoyed the small drama happening between the two of them: the hapless lover without a chance and the emotionally distant object of his affections.

"Knocked up," she said, then cussed.

"So what," her boy said. "Everything will be all right."

I gave them a stern face. "You shouldn't be smoking, not in your condition. Take care of your health."

"My sister, Nina, has a baby," Trina said, inhaling. "He's about five months. Her baby daddy comes over, gives her money and diapers, picks up the tot and makes funny noises, then leaves. He doesn't want to marry her but he sleeps with her regularly. Man, they get down. You can hear them through the wall, all over the house. My parents don't say nothing, as long as he is bringing money to support the kid. Still, after he leaves, she's so lonely that she goes to her room and cries almost all night."

"I'm sure that you don't want that kind of life," I said.

She passed the cigarette to the boy, who puffed on it right away. "My aunt says motherhood can be a downer. She said as soon as you have a baby that you cease to live for yourself anymore. It's all about the baby. I know my moms and my whole family, including my aunt, would help out a lot. She said she would help out with diapers, bottles, and wipes."

"I thought you wanted to get rid of it," the boy sneered.

"What's your name?" I asked him.

"Kite, that's my street name," the boy said. "I just don't want her to do something stupid. You're filling her head with some bull."

"I'm just asking her some questions, trying to get the lay of the land," I said. "Why don't you take Tarik's place and be the baby's father?"

"Don't play yourself, Holy Joe," Kite said angrily.

"Don't mess with him, K," the girl said. "He's just trying to make me see my whole situation. You said that Tarik wanted me to have an abortion because he had two other kids out there. You said they were costing him plenty and their baby mamas were loco."

Kite stubbed out the cigarette. "Shoot, Tarik is just like a lot of niggas. All they want to do is to smoke blunts and get some honeys to let them tap that body. Tarik just wants to make sure that Trina treats him right."

"And what is that?"

Kite grinned evilly. "He figures he has some rights as the father. He doesn't want to have her decide everything. He wants some say-so too about what is done with the baby. That's all he wants."

"Then he should be here and not out in the streets," I said. "He sent you to protect his interests, but I see how you're trying to muscle in on his woman. I think Trina sees it too."

Trina glared at him. "Tarik thinks he's a pretty boy. All the girls want him, right? He's nothing but a hood rat."

"I think you need a beat down," Kite growled.

"Maybe Tarik is playing both of you," I said. "I think he is giving you both a rotten deal. What are you going to do about school?"

"Holy Joe, you tripping," Kite shot back.

Trina thought about my school question. "My grades used to be good. I used to like school. Now, all of that book learning is for the birds. It's boring. I hate all them homework and the tests. But I didn't drop out because my parents would freak out."

"Education is crucial," I said. "Think it over. Think it over real good. Think of yourself and the baby. Don't let anybody sway you. You are the one carrying the baby. Sure, you got a lot on your plate but you can do this thing."

She looked at Kite and saw her future with him. "Oh man, I would stare at my belly and couldn't believe that there was something growing in there. It's unreal, this baby thing. When I told Tarik, he just grunted. That next morning, he sat up in his bed, walked to the bathroom naked, and came back, saying in this oily R. Kelly voice, 'I think we just made a rug rat.'"

"Do you want Tarik as your husband?" I asked.

"Heck no, " the girl said. "I don't believe him. I don't think he knows what he wants. First he says get rid of it, then he says if I do something to the baby, he'll mess me up. He's like most of these young niggas out here, very confused."

"That nigga ain't that crazy." Kite smiled, revealing a row of yellow, nicotine-stained teeth. "He loves females too much."

Then he lifted her sweater to expose her braless, full breasts, while crowing about her luscious, tasty breasts. He loved the expression of shock on my ashen face. He didn't take into account that I would be looking too. The girl yanked it down but not before I got a good look.

"Stop it." Trina was laughing.

"Trifling broad," Kite teased. "Reverend, you want her to settle down and find a good man to make her a respectable wifey. Ain't happening. Her fate is sealed."

I pointed at the door and yelled for Kite to leave. He rolled his yellow eyes at me and touched Trina on the shoulder gently. It was a tender gesture, but he meant the touch to send a signal to me. The touch said no matter what I said, his word was what carried the most weight to her.

"Please go," I said firmly.

After the door closed and we were alone, I pulled up a chair to face the girl, who was still laughing at the prank. My expression was solemn and grim.

"Are you high?" I asked her.

"Yes, I just had a couple of tokes before I came here," she replied. "I don't think it will hurt the baby. It's just weed, not crack or cheese."

"Weed is dope," I insisted. "It's not good for the baby."

"Not really," she said.

"Why do you let these boys treat you like this?" I said. "You're not a loose girl. They think you're easy. Respect yourself like a lady. On the other matter, I don't think Tarik will kill himself. He's just playing with your head. Mind games. Think of this. If you get the abortion, you will have to deal with the sting of that anguish of getting rid of the baby for the rest of your life. Abortion is nothing to play with. As a minister, I'll always see abortion as a wrong choice."

"Tarik said this baby will always come between us," she said. "How can he say this if he says he loves me? Can you believe he said this?"

I shrugged. "Everybody who loves you knows abortion is a bad choice. You will never get abortion out of your system. You will never forgive yourself."

"There's not too many guys to choose from in my neighborhood." She smirked. "It's a slum. Everybody's out of work. Everybody's on welfare. The folks around there are lazy and up to no good. I'm going crazy. I know if I didn't have this abortion, I'd have to live in shame and remorse."

"What frightens you the most?"

She snickered. "The darn rats. We had rats in the building. One big rat was under my covers on my bed. Crawling around my bare legs. I could feel its snout and little feet and long tail. I was screaming and screaming. I couldn't sleep at night in that bed. My father told the landlord to put down rat poison but one little kid across the hall got sick."

I frowned. "What do you want in your future?"

She stared ahead at the window, collecting her thoughts. "I guess I'll have to revise my game plan," she said.

"Give birth to the child," I said. "Raising the child is possibly the best thing you can do. Your parents, your relatives, your friends will support you in any choice you make. The initial disappointment and upset from your parents will diminish in time. I know this."

"Then I should be like Bristol Palin, the daughter of Sarah," she joked.

I laughed. "Not exactly. Do what's right."

"Yeah, but what is right, Reverend?"

I made my eyes soft and kind. "You can do this. You can do it with plenty of help and support. Our church is full of young mothers and their babies. They have a big support group with job training and GED classes. I know you can be a good mother. I know you are capable of raising a great child."

"If it wasn't Tarik's baby and it was someone else's, like my brother's," she said quietly, "would you still recommend I have it?"

"Is it your brother's baby?" I asked.

"No, just kidding," she said. "You know, dreams never come true for the poor, especially poor black girls. I don't need nobody. I can take care of my baby. I don't need a thing from nobody."

Then a knock sounded on the door. Hard pounding.

She got up. "When you get knocked up, you always got to pee. I hate that. All the time, pee, pee, pee."

Kite hugged her and they went off, whispering, and then he smacked her on her wide rear. Smiling, I watched them, these unruly kids, and muttered, "Life sometimes doesn't make sense."

CHAPTER 20

ABSOLUTELY NECESSARY

Be an example to the believers in word, in conduct, in spirit, in faith, in purity.
—1 Timothy 4:12

When it rains, it pours. Latrice, my sister, called me at both places: at the welfare agency office and at the church. I missed her usual call every two days. She would catch me up with the daily family gossip, deaths and weddings of our friends and relatives. There was a period of months when she went underground, often fleeing an abusive relationship following a failed restraining order.

Now, she had resurfaced and her man was arrested in a neighboring state for assault and robbery. He was a brute. She was finally free.

"How are you doing, big bro?" my sister said. "We haven't talked since you became a big hero but word has it that you're doing good work in the community. I want to see you."

"Sure, when are you in the city?" I asked. "Let's set something up."

The place for our brunch was a soul food restaurant, Red Velvet Cake Diner. Latrice knew the owner and figured she would get preferential treatment. As she said, they would treat us like family. I was trying to watch my waistline but I realized I could splurge on some treats and a few calories. We would meet at the place in the afternoon.

I arrived twenty minutes early, scoping out the place, seeing which seating was most favorable. The waitresses, a quartet of lovely black women, were very efficient, respecting every need of their patrons. One of them passed a menu to me as I lounged near the entrance, flashing a toothy smile at me.

When I turned, my sister was walking toward me, carrying a paper bag, laughing. I smiled at the musical tones of her delightful voice.

The waitress found us a table near the window facing the avenue. I pulled out the chair for her and remained standing until she was safely seated. She seemed genuinely pleased to see me.

"Hello, Clint," Latrice said, noticing my casual clothing.

"Sis, how are you?" I asked. "What do you have in the bag?"

"Blood oranges. I know you never liked them. Mom got me hooked on them. She always loved them when they were in season."

"Can I get you something?" the waitress asked, handing Latrice a menu. "A drink or coffee?"

"A cup of coffee for me," I said. "You want a cup?"

Latrice was thinner, not rail thin, but somewhat skeletal. She was a beautiful ashen ghost. Her hands trembled when she held the menu. I ignored the rasp in her voice.

"I'm doing all right," she said. "How are you doing?"

"Working hard, praying hard," I replied. "I still feel guilty now and then about Terry and the kids. I miss them terribly."

Her gray business suit hung off her like a sack. "You had some great years with her before it went sour," she said. "Everyone thought you guys would last forever. They thought you had the perfect marriage. What happened to you?"

"She became jealous of God," I answered.

"What do you mean?" she asked, motioning for the waitress. "She was never that petty. A little selfish, but not petty."

"She thought that I was spending too much time and energy in the service of the Lord, and gave me an ultimatum," I explained. "She told me that the church and the elders were playing me for a sucker. They, she added, were draining my youth and vitality and when they got finished with me, they would just throw me away."

"Do you believe that?"

"No." I shook my head.

My sister realized it was difficult for me to talk or think of my wife and the children. "Well, nothing could ever explain away what she did to the kids and to herself. I don't think she fully thought what her actions would do to you."

"I do . . . all right," I stuttered. "I'm blessed to be still standing."

She gave me one of her more serious looks. "I know I'm blessed. I don't know if you knew Bettye Bass, one of the girls we grew up with. She was a cheerleader just like I was. She was married to a soldier just back from Japan. I got a call from her mother who said she died last Wednesday."

"The woman with the pretty green eyes and those great long legs," I joked. "She was a stunner. I remember her."

"Bettye died from breast cancer," she said in a firm voice. "We got diagnosed at about the same time. I used to stay in touch with her during her treatments but then she dropped out of sight. I knew she had an uphill fight after that diagnosis of stage-three breast cancer."

"Oh God, I hope she didn't have any children," I volunteered. "That's going to be rough for them."

"She had three kids. Her husband is a sweetheart. He supported her through everything. He was right there through the end. I know she did some appearances for the breast cancer awareness campaign. She walked every walk and was once the grand marshal."

"How are you doing?"

"Like I said I'm blessed, you know there is no history of cancer in our family," she said. "I got my regular mammogram and it was clear. But I found a lump in my right breast about three weeks after that. My husband said I should go and get another mammogram. I really didn't want to do it. I hate getting my breasts flattened out. It's so uncomfortable."

The waitress drifted near the table, glancing at us, but we shooed her away. We needed time. Besides, I had never heard the story of how she almost botched her early detection of the cancer. One doctor said there was nothing to fear since 80 percent of lumps are benign.

"If I had waited for that second mammogram, I would be dead," she said, her eyes frozen. "I paid attention to my body and now I will survive. The biopsy showed a tumor, which had gone into an advanced stage of cancer. I needed a second or third opinion. I switched doctors and this one told me that a treatment regimen of chemo and radiation might do the trick."

"Oh boy, you must have been scared out of your mind."

She cocked her head and permitted me to see her slide the wig on her pretty head. "I was scared shitless. Three lymph nodes under my arm were inflamed. I just knew I was going to die."

My sister examined the menu with its sumptuous brunch of grits, eggs, home fries, waffles, pancakes, biscuits, turkey bacon, beef sausage, and country ham. Meanwhile, I looked at the other items like the smothered chicken, BBQ half chicken, fried catfish, salmon cakes, coleslaw, potato salad, and homemade corn bread.

"I'll do the regular brunch," I said. "Grits, salmon cakes, and scrambled eggs. Biscuits. What about you?"

"The same," she agreed. The complications from the chemo gave her a queasy stomach, headaches, and insomnia.

"It's so nice to see you," I said, smiling. I put my hand over her bony fingers. "We've got to do this more often."

"I should keep on my low-fat diet to stay on the right track," she said. "One of the women from my support group said African American women get more cancer than any other race under age forty. We also die at a faster rate than white women of the same age. The cancers are much more aggressive so we must be more vigilant."

"Do you exercise?"

"Not yet. The oncologist said to go slow with this cancer."

I gently removed my hand from hers and wiped a tear from her cheek. This was getting very sad and painful. The sides attracted my attention: macaroni and cheese, candied yams, rice and peas, collard greens, cabbage, string beans, cornbread stuffing, and garden green salad. Everything looked good. We watched the waitresses scurry about, with trays laden with aromatic food, to their patrons.

"This place is awesome," she said. "I wish I lived near here."

I didn't look up from the menu. Desserts. Coconut cake, sweet potato pie, chocolate layer cake, banana pudding, carrot cake, pecan pie, lemon cake, sweet potato cheesecake, and their signature red velvet cake.

"No, you don't, because you would be big as a house," I teased. "I don't know how anybody can keep a decent waistline when you eat all of this food. You would be big as a blimp."

We both laughed like children chuckling at a bit of family gossip.

She commented that I rarely smiled when I was married and dealing with Terry's mess, but now a grin was always plastered on my face. I had endured a battle of wits with my wife and lost.

"Why are you so at ease, Clint?" she asked. "Are you in love?"

"No, not at all."

She peered at my face. "Are you dating? Is there somebody special in your life?"

I ignored her and watched the waitresses gather at the front counter. My sister took the hint.

She laughed through her tears. She remembered me as a young boy trying to teach my puppy how to talk and read. She remembered me carrying my prized baseball glove everywhere I went. She remembered my sweet tooth, how I loved my grandma's hot blackberry cobbler topped with homemade vanilla ice cream.

When she reminded me of my childhood antics, I smiled and admitted the accuracy of her memory. I

watched the diners lining up for seats and the wonderful meals. After the waitress took our order, it was no
time before she delivered the food.

"They took both of my breasts and scooped away the
cancerous cells and the remaining breast tissue," she
said. "They did reconstructive surgery on my chest. My
husband is wonderful. He accepts the hideous scars on
my chest, the good and bad days, and the rigid schedule of my treatments."

"A lot of men would have run," I said. My mouth was
dry and my stomach felt sick. I wondered if my wife
would have remained throughout a health crisis.

"Yes, he loves me." She grinned. "Thank God."

I took a forkful of fluffy grits, buttery and seasoned
just right, and put it in my mouth. "I wish I had that
kind of love in our marriage. Instead, Terry was very
possessive and jealous of everything that touched our
family. She felt that she was no longer the center of our
universe. I couldn't believe she was even jealous of my
spirituality."

"Terry was a control freak," my sister insisted. "She
always wanted to be top dog. I talked to her mother at
the funeral and she said she was always like that."

"My wife and I got on each other's nerves," I said.
"When I first met Terry, I wasn't looking for a wife. In
fact, I don't know what I was looking for. She was so
psychologically complex. You know what I was like at
that time. She really felt that I was clueless about how
to keep her happy and she was right. I failed."

"I never understood why you chose Terry in the first
place," she said. "She didn't like your family or your
background."

"What do you mean?"

"Remember how she used to act around our parents?
I think she thought you were beneath her. A com-

moner. Like she was marrying down. She didn't feel anybody was her intellectual equal, too, because she had college degrees from an Ivy League school."

I speared a bite of the tasty salmon. "I was mesmerized by her beauty and sexuality. She seemed so stylish. I think she liked my clumsiness at first, but it drove her crazy. She wanted me to be a great ladies' man. She wanted me to be something I wasn't. In all of the time that we were together, I don't think she ever committed to me or our family."

"That was her loss," she retorted. "It was a bad partnership."

"In the beginning, I saw Terry as a complete person with smarts, elegance, personality, and accomplishments. She saw our relationship as a war of wills. Winners and losers. She had to come out on top. I knew she was more experienced than me. I just wanted her to be honest about what she was thinking, what she was doing."

"Did you have an open marriage?"

"I didn't consider our marriage that. I only thought Terry was confused. I realized early on that I had gotten in over my head."

"Terry told me every man she dated wanted to do her," my sister said, toying with the highly seasoned eggs. "They all wanted to take her to bed and she obliged them. She thought you were a 'tragic clown.' Those were her words. She said you didn't have a roving eye. You weren't like the regular guys. She wanted you to compete with her, wanted you to get the balls to confront her."

"How could I? I was a minister. I pledged myself to God."

"Clint, she saw you as a joke," she added. "She heard some of your fellow clergy brothers razz you about lack of your sexual aggression. They thought you didn't like females."

"That's crazy," I grumbled. "I didn't want to jeopardize my marriage and my family. I knew she wanted out. I was a mental and physical wreck. I didn't want to lose my family. Above all things, I didn't want to lose Terry."

"I'm sorry that I brought this up."

I stopped eating and put the pack of cigarettes on the table. I just stared at the patrons and the cars and trucks going past in the street. The expression on my face reflected the bitterness and torment inside my heart.

"You can't smoke that in here, Clint." She sipped her water.

"People do make mistakes," I said quietly. "Lord only knows what she was going through in her mind. As Dr. Smart would say, it was a collapse of character, and maybe so. Maybe suppressed rage. But I know she was emotionally hurt, injured deeply, and she made some bad errors in judgment."

"You always let her off the hook," she snapped. "What else have you been up to?"

I looked around again, frowning. "I let a young boy down. And he killed himself. That's the latest of my screw-ups."

"Clint, you were always hard on yourself," she said. "Even as a boy, you always took things on and internalized them. You cannot save the world."

"I know but I could have been there when he needed me. A troubled boy . . . He reached out for help . . . to anybody . . . to his mother . . . to me and we failed him. He was coming to the youth program at the church. His mother realized he needed help but she didn't know how to rescue him. None of us did."

Her expression was utterly serious, considering my doomed, loveless marriage and now this sacrificed boy. I was headed for further misery. She would appeal to my desire to survive and to heal. She knew I was not a spineless man.

"The kids these days look death in the face every day and they have a different attitude toward it," she said. "They plan their own funerals. They know how they want the burial service to be, what they will wear, what songs will be played. All down to the last detail. You know what I mean."

I glanced up at her from the plate. "Yeah, this is a totally different world today from when we were coming up. I really don't understand it."

"Neither do I." She heard my dry chuckle.

"So what do I do about this woman I met?" I laughed again.

"All right, a woman, now you're cooking." She perked up. "How long has this been going on?"

"Very recently. I think I like her."

She gave me a conspiratorial smile. "I love it. I know it. My brother is back out in the singles scene. You've got to think single, act single. You're a widower but you don't have to act like one."

"I don't know about acting single," I said.

"You'll learn quick enough." My sister laughed. "It's like getting back on the bicycle. Dating is an art."

"Yeah, right."

"Don't make the same mistakes that you made with Terry," she said. "Not every woman who wiggles her hips is worth your time. Set some rules about this thing. Know what you want. And don't take anything less. Don't let your date know all your business on the first date. Keep them guessing."

I nodded my head. My sister was right, for once.

"Find somebody who likes the same things you do. Don't get some female up in your life and let her disrupt it. Choose the women you get close with and let them know you are the boss. You run the show. Even if you're heated up by her, don't let her know it. Don't be too eager."

"It's been awhile since I've dated," I admitted.

"Is the woman married or attached?" she asked.

"No, I don't think so."

"Think of this," she added. "If a woman is willing to step out on her man, how can you respect her? She has the morals of an alley cat. She might be easy with you and everybody else. You know what I mean?"

"Yes, I do." I played with the butter knife.

She winked. "Have you made any moves?"

"Not yet, just a polite collection of kisses." I grinned. "But I will."

Her smile was luminous. "Listen to that little voice in the back of your head. Never go against that. If that voice starts yelling, you need to step away and leave the woman alone."

"I know that."

"You didn't listen to it when you found Terry, and you paid for it," she said softly. "You don't need a repeat engagement."

"I know, I know."

"And if it gets hot and heavy, use a rubber," my sister reminded me. "You've not been out here for a while. The dating scene is very serious. The rules have changed. Every time you have sex, you're putting your life on the line. Protect yourself."

My sister wanted to build a fence around me, so I wouldn't get hurt. But I was a big boy and I needed to get back out there. I wanted to see the dating situation very clearly. At least the object of my affection was not a skeptic. At least Miss Collier was not unsympathetic toward all things spiritual or religious. I could work with that.

CHAPTER 21

SOME FEMININE LOGIC

Faithful are the wounds of a friend; but the kisses of an enemy are deceitful.
—Proverbs 27:6

Thinking back on the brunch with my sister, Latrice, she made it clear that I must leave the tragedy behind to survive. As the Southern novelist Katherine Anne Porter once put it regarding the moments in the rearview mirror, she wrote: "The past is never where you think you left it."

So true, I thought. *I must be very honest about the situation with Terry and the murders so I won't go from one crisis to the next.* I was tired of hiding out. Everybody seemed to say I must think about my life in a new way. Starting over can be done. A new beginning. Since the funerals, I was crippled by self-doubt and indecision as I was leery of making choices. I kept putting them off even if it meant that other people began deciding for me.

Life was not finished. I could bounce back from the brink and learn the tough lessons of life and apply them to the days ahead.

"I had a wonderful time today." My sister called that evening. "We haven't had a talk like that in a while. I was always so close to you, more than anybody else in our family."

"I enjoyed it too. I think I'm ready to move on now. I can't lie to myself. Now I've got to get up and go forward."

I realized that I was avoiding the emotional pain by working around the clock. Some people do it with alcohol, sex, drugs, bad rebound relationships, keeping by themselves, or meaningless activities. I smothered the pain by working.

"I'm glad that you talked about Terry today," she said. "This is the first time you admitted a lot of things to yourself. Everybody wanted you to get therapy but I knew you would come around someday. I told our kin folks that you didn't need a shrink. You had the Lord who would guide you through."

"That's true."

In my mind, I didn't know whether I had resolved the puzzle of Terry yet. I kept looking at her from all angles. She was always spying on me during our marriage. Keeping tabs on me. She really didn't trust me. I was never alone. After all of our fights and squabbles, I discovered I didn't care about who or what she did. She was a selfish little girl in a woman's body.

"What about this other woman?" my sister asked. "Miss Collier."

"You mean Claire, right?" I forgot I'd mentioned her at brunch.

"Yes. When are you going to make your move? Human beings are not meant to be alone or they start acting dumb. You know what I mean?"

I was laying out my evening clothes. "Yes, I do."

"Sometimes you can think too much, too." She chuckled.

"I'm going over there later on tonight," I said.

Following the phone call from my sister, I showered, washed my hair, and shaved closely. I made a show of

confidence when I examined my image in the bathroom mirror but I knew the spirit, and flesh can be a
weak thing. Fragile. Extremely vulnerable. Still, I could
not live like I was living, stuck in this rigid environment of shame and guilt.

*Do I love the Lord too much? Is it interfering with
my life? Is there something wrong with me, like Terry
said?*

In the strong bathroom light, I brushed back the
stray hairs of my mustache and checked my finger-
nails. *Is something wrong with me?*

Later, on the way to Claire's apartment, I tried to
reassure myself with rehearsed lines, ego-boosting
phrases, comic winks, and practiced cocky smiles. It
was like I was going on my first high school date. I had
been on the sidelines in the romance wars for so long.

However, when I arrived there, I was my old self, the
former Clint before the arrival of Terry in my life, before my failed marriage, before the painful tragedy that
cost me my children. Claire offered me a glass of wine
to settle me down.

"How's traffic out there?" she asked. She was wearing a skin-tight short black dress, worn to achieve the
desired effect.

"Very light." I noticed how she buzzed about in the
room. She pivoted, swaying her bottom. I stared at her
butt, knowing that was sinful behavior. But somehow
that didn't matter now.

"I noticed you don't talk much," she said. "I saw that
right away. You're not one of those chatty guys. I hate
that. Some men feel they have to run off at the mouth
all the time."

I sat on the sofa, raised the drink to my lips, and set
it down on the table. The old-timey preachers didn't resist sin and temptation. They welcomed it. They always

wanted to take on Satan, go and do battle with him toe-to-toe. I realized Satan was the master of transformation, able to deceive and demonize, able to weave a dark spell over a person.

No matter how spiritual or religious, I felt disoriented. I felt peculiar, as if I was aware of my body for the first time since Terry's death. I felt like I didn't belong there in that room, in that apartment. This was not Terry, my wife, but another woman. I didn't belong there.

"You're a real scoundrel, aren't you?" she asked.

"Not really."

She cackled. "How does it feel to be a representative of God?"

"I do my best but sometimes I fall short." I was very aware I was a man and very much a sinner.

"What gives you the right to act as a divine messenger of the Holy Word?" she asked, drinking her drink.

"God called me." I was getting nervous.

"Called you how? By phone or a burning bush?"

"This is not a joking matter," I said. "Maybe I made a mistake coming over here. I thought we could just talk a little and get to know each other. I didn't expect this."

"Expect what?"

"This intense questioning," I said, lighting a cigarette. "An interrogation."

"So what gives you the right to save souls?"

I smoked the cigarette quietly, exhaling through the nose. "Why are you asking these questions? I turned to you for comfort and serenity. I hoped you would be a safe harbor. I must confess that I'm a little uneasy being here. This is a very, very shaky period in my life."

"Like I'm not," Claire flared up. "I just lost a child."

She was on a rampage. The temporary fit of temper started to grow into an ongoing bad mood and she kept getting madder, madder, and madder. I couldn't figure her out.

"Why can't you just be friendly?" she added. "I want nothing from you."

I thought about leaving right then and there. However, I could see my sister's stern face and hear her words that I should see where the evening went. *Try to break free of the gloom.*

The rings of her cell phone were muffled by the leather thickness of her purse. I didn't belong here. She reached for it and took the call into the hallway. From there, she became agitated by the caller and locked herself in the bathroom. I was now extremely nervous. She talked for several minutes, her reedy voice traveled through the door, but I could only make out various nasty phrases and disjointed words.

She walked out of the bathroom and slammed the phone down on the table. "Somehow I get the feeling that you're enjoying all of this. Just sitting there and laughing at me. Judging me and all that."

"I can't judge anybody," I replied. "I'm not God."

She emptied her glass and wiped her mouth with a napkin. "I was told that you're a real scoundrel. I hope you live up to your reputation. Maybe I need a little distraction. I'm bored. Sometimes I surprise myself. Sometimes I want what I shouldn't have."

"Sometimes I think you just like to hear yourself talk," I shot back. "I think you're in love with the sound of your own voice."

With my retort, she mumbled a curse. For the first time, I noticed her hair was wet and slicked back. No makeup.

"Tell me what you need, Miss Collier."

"Call me Claire," she said firmly. "I told you that."

Frowning, she became angry, enraged at the idea of any need being fulfilled by somebody outside herself. She went berserk. Her hand sent the glass flying against the wall, shattering it into shards in a loud explosion.

"What do you need, Claire?" I asked calmly.

There was complete silence from me. I could see the desire and lust in her eyes. I decided to take three sips of wine. It had been awhile since I last drank. The last time was when my family was wiped out.

"What keeps you going, Reverend?" she asked, watching me.

"Knowing God is a good God." I smiled. "That's all."

"He took the only thing I cared about," she sneered. "I thought if I believed in Him that He would protect me. I didn't think He would hurt me this way. I didn't do anything to get on God's bad side."

"I know," I agreed, taking another sip. It was just wine, not whiskey.

The drink clouded my head yet I knew I possessed something she wanted. She glared at me as if she demanded I make the first move. Be the aggressor. I was stunned at the sheer force of the physical attraction with my entire body tingling in anticipation.

"Do you think my butt is too big?"

I replied slowly. "Just right."

She poured me another drink, tilting her head curiously. "Do you trust me? Will you put yourself in my hands?"

"I don't know about that." I eyed her as I drank.

She clicked her tongue. "What a pity. We could have so much fun."

"I didn't come up here for that," I said firmly.

"Don't be a wuss," she said, her face near my neck.

"I'm not." *Ah, the opposite sex.*

There was that magical moment when she locked eyes with mine. I felt my body temperature rising as I reached out and touched her for the first time. I reached under the short black dress, expecting the silky barrier of panties, but they were absent.

"I lost my virginity to a man like you," she purred.

I was old enough to know my own mind; I wanted her in the worst way. As she knelt down, my fingers stroked the soft skin of her shoulder.

"You smell good, Reverend," she said, sniffing the spark of my pent-up excitement. She wanted to pull me up into a wet kiss but she didn't dare.

"I can't do this," I protested. Her fingers on my body sent a shudder through me. I knew the sex between us would be astounding, even incredible.

She stood up in all of her majesty, in all her splendor. I was transfixed when she removed her clothes. I hadn't seen a naked woman in some time. My eyes drank in every delectable curve, every delicious hillock, every desirable mound. I was very self-conscious about being nude in front of a strange woman other than Terry. *Dead Terry.*

"I'm going to ride you, cowboy," Claire said in a rough voice.

Downright nervous, I looked down at my arousal and we both exploded in laughter.

"Reverend, where have you been, prison?" She laughed.

"Sort of," I replied, also laughing. I was drowning in sweat.

But after a few harmless kisses and hugs, we sat there on the sofa, her head on my shoulder, not talking. Nothing happened. I didn't want to seduce her. I didn't want to do any heavy petting. After all, I was a Christian and a minister in good standing. I could never forget those things.

Claire had a wicked grin on her face while she made plans for me to enter her life. Every day, every night, every moment. She'd make me forget all about my dead wife and my murdered kids, if I let her. But it was hard to let that love for Terry go.

CHAPTER 22

FLAT ON HIS BACK

All of them pleased God because of their faith.
But still they died without given what had been
promised.
                                        —Hebrews 11: 39

"My chest doesn't hurt so bad now that the docs gave me this super-duper medicine," my father said between gasps. "They said I dodged the big one." He'd collapsed near the poultry section of the local grocery market, fell against his cart and rolled onto the floor, and they rushed him to the hospital.

It turned out that there had been a dull pain in his left arm for days but he ignored it. My mother told him to go to the doctor. She complained he was working too hard and not getting enough sleep. When you get older, you cannot always do what you could when you were young. My father didn't understand that.

I walked closer to his bed, noticing that there was a heart monitor wired to his chest. The heartbeat seemed steady and strong. He was embarrassed by his family seeing him like this, weak and disabled, not able to roar. My sister didn't come. They had been fighting over the last three weeks. I tried to get her to visit him. She was as stubborn as he was.

"The docs said I've got to cut out the junk food, liquor, cigars, and anything with a lot of calories," he grumbled. "They want to take all of the fun out of my life. Heck, I might as well be dead."

"Don't say that, honey," my mother said. She looked worried.

"You'll get better in no time, Dad," I added. "They just think you got to change some of your habits. Whatever the doctors ask you to do, you've got to do it if you want to get well."

There was a look in the eyes of my father that I'd never seen before. It was the look of somebody who had been brushed by the dark wings of death and lived to tell about it. He was scared. He'd seen his mortality and realized what all humans know.

"They had this older woman in here just now," he said, his eyes going to an empty bed. "She was brought in here about four hours ago. She fainted during a ceremony where the mayor was giving her a citation. The woman had raised fifty foster kids in her home. They said all of the kids turned out right."

My mother interrupted. "So have our kids."

"I don't know about that," the old man sneered. "We were talking after her family left for the night. She was telling me about loving the kids just like they were hers. See, she couldn't have any kids. Something was wrong with her down there. She told me the kids changed her life and maybe she changed theirs."

"Bless her heart," my mother said.

"I asked her if she did it for the cash; taking in foster kids can be a money-making business." He laughed. "But she said she didn't do it because of the money, but because she loved the kids. It wasn't about a fast buck for her."

"Some people are just goodhearted," I noted. "We need more people like them. Like her. It would be a totally different world."

"You would say that, Mr. Softie." He grinned, scoring a point. "I asked her about whether her husband went along with her scam. She said he did. He loved the kids too."

"Why do you believe the worst in everybody?" I asked.

"Because human beings are basically evil," my father replied. "They sin. They do bad things. They don't care about others."

"Where is the woman now?" my mother asked.

"She's dead." He nodded as if that was a good thing. "Her heart just gave out. They took her away."

I stood near the doorway and watched the interns and residents moving in a steady stream of white. The tension in the room was serious. With a fast gait, my father's doctor, a skinny, nervous white man with zits, came into the room with an intern and a nurse. My mother said the doctor seemed to know his stuff.

"How are you, sir?" the doctor asked him. "How's the pain in your chest?"

"Better," my father replied. I noticed he loved the attention.

"Did the meds help alleviate it somewhat?"

"Yes, they did."

His doctor did his business with the stethoscope, checking the old man's pulse, and watching the heart monitor. "We want your family to know that the standard chest pain workup will be done. There will also be the EKG, chest X-ray, and routine lab tests completed as well. I want to know the extent of the cardiac risk factors. Believe me, we will be very detailed."

I thought of the cardiac risk factors my father possessed. He smoked four cigars daily, and even more stogies when his wife wasn't looking.

"Hopefully, the heart wasn't damaged a lot," the doctor said. "That is what we want to find out."

"As a black man, he has to be much more careful with health," the eager intern interrupted. "Most black men have a life expectancy of sixty-nine years, much shorter than white men and males of other races. They fall victim to lung disease, cancer, hypertension, heart disease, stroke, and diabetes. We don't want him to become a statistic."

"And he won't," my father's doctor added.

I grinned at the old man. This was the first time he had been admitted in the hospital in years.

"Now, I'm going to have you folks leave so he can get some rest," the doctor said, waving us out. He pulled us aside, telling us he'd talk to the family when the results were in.

The following day, the same doctor called us into his office. We were expecting bad news. On the way over to the hospital, my mother and I discussed how my father was in denial about his health, and that he was truly a very sick man. He would never be the same robust man he was just ten years ago.

The doctor welcomed us into the room, inviting us to be seated. He joked about my father trying to bribe a candy striper into sneaking a beer into his room. That scheme was foiled.

"Now, your husband has minimal heart damage and that is the plus side." The doctor addressed my mother. "The EKG was slightly irregular but not drastic. There might be a leaky valve involved. However, the blood work was fine."

"When can we take him home?" my mother asked.

"We'd like to hold him for few more days or so, run some more tests, and adjust his meds to suit his particular problem," the doctor said. "Your husband has got to change his diet, stress levels, and sleeping patterns. He needs rest, rest, rest."

"Don't worry, we'll see that he gets the rest he needs," I offered.

Back in his room, a nurse was tinkering with the monitor and fluffing his pillow behind his head. She gave him two pills and a paper cup of water. He swallowed the meds, meek as a lamb.

"When are they going to let me out of here?" he asked her.

"Sometime at the end of the week," I answered for the nurse. "They still have to do some more tests. They want to make sure your chest pain goes away. But you'll have to take the medicine they give you."

"I'll get on his butt if he doesn't." My mother laughed. She was happy that the news was not grim. This was something she could handle.

"You didn't forget that we talked about this before," he said. "Bad choices and wrong judgments can ruin a person. Everybody has their daily challenges. Suffering touches us all."

My mother looked at him, then at me. "What is he talking about?"

"Grief can be a tonic," my father said. "Use it."

I shook my head. Even on his sickbed, he could be cruel and nasty.

"What are you talking about?" my mother repeated.

"I told my son he was a loser," he sneered. "We had a little talk about the need of the living to remember the dead. He knows what I said to him."

The nurse smiled. "He'll be asleep soon. The meds will put him out for hours. He needs his rest."

I walked to the window and looked at the ambulance pulling into the receiving bay of the emergency room. Two attendants jumped out and pulled out an elderly woman on a stretcher.

Touching my sleeve, my mother whispered that my father hadn't rested for hours. He had been extremely fitful and agitated. We turned back to the patient, where he was snoring lightly with his fists clenched.

I remembered a T-shirt of one of the young girls from the group, yellow with red letters across the chest: HOME IS WHERE THE HEARTBREAK IS. That brought a smile to my face. I wondered how my father would act back in the real world with the health scare.

CHAPTER 23

A SOUL'S TREK

By faith, Abraham obeyed when he was called . . .
He went out, not knowing where he was going.
                                                    —Hebrews 11:8

"'You can develop a healthy, robust community that lives right with God and enjoys its results only if you do the hard work of getting along with each other, treating each other with dignity and respect.'" I stood on the pulpit steps, my mouth open in praise, my arms outstretched to the heavens.

The organist gave a little supporting riff to boost the power of my words of devotion. A few members of the congregation said, "Amen" and asked me to teach the Holy Word of the Lord. Some of the elders shifted in their seats nervously because I was getting off course.

"The disciple James wrote that basic truth in the third chapter and the eighteenth verse," I said with a sudden fury. "He was talking to us. He was talking to us who know better. Everybody in this church knows better than to treat the people in this community worse than you would wish to be treated."

A man, a senior deacon, strolled up the aisle, crying, "Teach it, brother! Teach it!"

I surveyed the congregation of this modest church across the railroad tracks, in a bad neighborhood of dingy slum buildings. When Dr. Smart requested my services in going across town to sub for him, he knew the church's reputation as one of the finest places to worship in one of the worst parts of the city. Packed into the meeting hall, the faithful filled the pews, their Sunday best on their bodies, and now there were stragglers in folding chairs set up in the aisles.

"God is a just God," I shouted. "God knows what we are doing. He knows who is living right, knows who needs to be saved, knows who needs to be redeemed. We can read the blessed Old Testament and New Testament, but if we do not practice God's sacred Word outside of church, but if we are sinning, drinking, whoring, lying, cursing, doing everything that would earn us a place in hell, then we are lost. Hell will be our permanent home. Permanent, not for a week or two days!"

The church erupted with waves and waves of adoration and praise for me, this young messenger of the Word. I fell silent, and walked dramatically to the altar near the large golden cross with the crucified Savior on it, my face in a tortured expression of pain and sorrow.

"The text for today is whether our community will choose between faith and freedom or foolishness and failure," I said, and then repeated my thesis, pointing toward the suffering Christ. "All He requires is that we become hard workers in the Temple of the Lord. If we do that, our community will prosper. If we obey His will, our community will thrive."

Two of the old sisters, long-time members, shouted for the truth to be taught. One of the choir members yelled that God is never dead. However, the church's pastor looked at the large banner that hung across the pulpit: THE SAVIOR REDEEMS ALL SINNERS.

"There can be no vanity in the faithful," I said, noticing his gaze. "We can all say that we are unworthy. We are unworthy to receive His blessing. We must have faith, a strong and powerful faith, in Christ, which will let us do all His good works. This mighty faith in the Lord whose blood has cleansed us from all sin will deliver us."

Again and again the organist's agile fingers lifted the solemn words of my sermon up into the rafters of the church, soaring among the lyrics of the old sacred hymns sung by the faithful. Those who knew that they had lived lives short of the glory of God sang the loudest and boldest.

"Praise the Lord," Reverend Childs said, supporting my words.

"Praise the Lord," a group of the elders said, perched high in gilded chairs on the raised platform near the pulpit. Another of the choir struck a few percussive notes on the tambourine, adding a joyous sound to my preaching.

"Amen, amen, amen," echoed the deacons in unison.

"Faith will make you free, will set you free," I said. "God rewards the faithful. God gives salvation and eternal life to people who don't earn it. God gives it to those who don't deserve it. God gives us sinners His love and forgiveness. I thank Him for loving and forgiving me. I thank Him for his undying support. We need His love and forgiveness for our community."

"Amen, brother, amen," yelled one of the parishioners, suddenly jumping up.

I slyly grinned and continued speaking with the organist sprinkling dark and solemn notes underneath my ideas of redemption. "Faith allows us to struggle

valiantly from our birth until our death with the power
of sin within our soul," I said. "Faith permits us to control our sins. Faith directs us away from vice, lust, and
evil."

"Teach, young man," bellowed Sister Duncan, fan-
ning herself with one of the funeral fans. She was a
hefty sister and the deacons prayed that she would not
fall out. Nobody wanted to carry her to the comfort of
the basement. They watched her gyrating until the fe-
ver of the Spirit passed through her.

I walked right up to the congregation and smiled
broadly at them. No one in the church knew what I
would do next.

"Faith is a strong weapon of the heart and soul," I
said, waving the Bible. "We know that God will provide
us strength and guidance to deal with any situation put
before us. Let me say this. If God had not fortified my
faith, I would not be here before you now. I had slipped,
tripped, and fallen into the dark pit of depression."

"We know your loss, brother," Reverend Childs shouted. "You can testify for God's grace. You know firsthand.
You know what the Lord has done for you."

I turned toward the church's minister and wiped away
a tear. "I believed deep in my heart that the Lord would
give me the strength to handle my grief. I believed God
would be with me and in me. I knew He would not fail
me. I knew He would not leave me alone. I knew He
would not make me fend for myself in those dark times."

"Praise the Lord," the deacons said in harmony.

"When you have that faith, that gift of faith, the Lord
shines His presence within us and works within us," I
said. "Once He does that, we become more compassionate, more accepting people. We become kinder, tolerant,
generous. That's what being a Christian means."

"You're definitely one of the faithful, brother," one of the deacons shouted. "Look at all of your good works. Look at what you have done for so many people."

"It's not my will, but Thy will that has made everything come to pass," I said. "It's the presence of the Lord. He has stayed the hand of Satan and not made me bitter and hard. He has allowed me to live again and love again."

As I said this personal insight, I thought about how Dr. Smart's sermons were like a readable CliffsNotes on the Bible: more folksy and close to the essence of the Scripture. However, the sermons of Reverend Childs were socially aware, sometimes political, and very intellectually astute. I remembered when Reverend Childs and Dr. Smart and others organized their members to whitewash local billboards with dangerous liquor and tobacco ads. That was five years ago.

"Lord, have mercy," a sister shouted, waving her hand.

"I ask you members, the faithful: what is the will of the Lord?" I asked. "What does He want from us as the saved, the faithful?"

A great cry of joy filled the church as the members embraced the teachings of the Holy Ghost. They shouted that they were the men and women of God. They shouted a series of "amens" and "Praise the Son of God."

I walked up the center aisle and continued talking about the way of the righteous. "The Bible must be a living document and our faith must be our holy touchstone. Love for the Living God and our abiding faith are the only ways to the renewal of the soul."

"Teach it, teach it," cried the congregation.

"Freedom is a state of mind," I said. "We don't want to be free. We don't want to think and don't want to find out this truth outside of the church, out in our homes, in our families, in our communities. We treat our children, our future, like they don't matter. Every day we see the tragedy played out in the newspapers and on the television that we have harmed our young, even killed them. And you wonder why we are afraid of them."

The entire church was silent. You could hear some of the elderly breathe. Even the noisy organist became quiet, leaning forward to hear the pastor.

"God doesn't accept our present way of living, our fighting, our destroying each other," I went on. "Above our elders, above our children, above our families, above our community, we place money, fancy clothes, sex, things, and fast cars instead of serving the Lord. The righteous life has a purpose. Forsake your desires, urges, wants, and prejudices. Free your heart and soul with the blood of Jesus."

The congregation was hanging on to my every word, my every indictment of them. I immediately thought, *they will not be inviting me back anytime soon, but I must speak from the heart.*

"I'm tired of hearing it's the white folks who makes us act this way to one another," I said. "No . . . no . . . no. It is us. We must be honest about our shortcomings. We must respect ourselves before we can get the respect of others. We are acting like little children. We must decide if we're fearless in Christ or scared children."

One or two members clapped but the rest remained quiet.

The church's pastor and his deacons gave me the evil eye and shook their heads. This was not in the program. They were afraid that I would go militant or too black on them. That was not my agenda.

I pointed to the congregation, shouting and thrusting the Holy Book up high. "I challenge you to be true Christians. I challenge you the faithful to live like the Lord wants. Be responsible. Be moral. And be free."

Then I turned and walked back to the pulpit. There was a delayed reaction until the church suddenly erupted with high praise and clapping and the choir sang at full throat some of the old hymns. I sat among the elders, cradling my frayed Bible, and Reverend Childs reached down and shook my hand. A group of the deacons, sensing that everything was all right, also lined up to shake my hand. It was one of my greatest triumphs spreading the Word of the Lord.

CHAPTER 24

WE AS ONE

Your faith should not be in the wisdom of men but in the power of the Lord.
—1 Corinthians 2:5

After the stunning service at the church, I walked in the city park, noticing the groups of teen boys and men with their sagging pants, pit bulls, and Rottweilers. They passed around bottles of beer and wine among them. I could smell the desperation and rage on them. Some of them wore hoodies and pants all off their butts.

As a cop car cruised past them, the two white patrolmen stared at the group, eyeing them for inappropriate behavior. Three of the boys gave them the finger and yelled out curses, taunting the police.

I took off my jacket, watching the tense situation, and sat on a bench. The police car slowed and did a U-turn. Some of the adults rubbed their crotches while a couple of lean young females walked by them, dressed in very tight jeans and revealing tops featuring their curves.

"Hey, cutie, why don't you let me do you?" one of the boys yelled at the girls. "You know you want it."

Another of the adults, holding up a bottle, shouted: "Here's to fresh honeys everywhere! Let me break your seal, hottie."

The girls hurried past the insults and humiliations while the policemen parked, their hands on their pistols, and stood outside the car. They seemed definitely afraid and wanted to be anywhere other than the park.

Angry, I got up and walked away quickly. "You need to provide those girls with protection, Officers," I said as I neared the policemen. One of them waved me off.

That evening, Dr. Smart called and congratulated me for the sermon delivered at the church. I was distracted by my discovery of Terry's favorite piece of jewelry that day, a string of pearls, on the bathroom sink. I knew there was no way that I had left the pearls there. The pearls just appeared there as if by magic. I had given up trying to figure out what the meaning was of the pearls' appearance. *Odd things happen.*

"Reverend Childs says you captivated the congregation," the old man crowed. "He was so excited by the response of the parishioners to you. I'm really glad that I sent you."

I smiled ear to ear. "I'm glad you sent me too."

"Brother Clint, you've made a brilliant comeback. Not everybody could have come back like you did. I know it was rocky for a while there but you put your trust and faith in the Lord and He led you through."

"Yes, He did," I agreed.

"I'm so proud of you, Clint."

"Thank you, sir." I was still grinning.

"All eyes in the religious community are on you," Dr. Smart said, his voice low and easy. "Everybody knows what you have come through. They sympathize with you having lost everything that you love and clinging to the powerful faith of Jesus Christ to pull you through. You are a true saint."

"Not really," I said. I knew better than to overestimate my importance.

"I have a little task for you to do this week," the old man said. "I know I've been putting you through your paces in recent weeks but it's good for you. Keeps your mind off your problems."

"Or creates new ones." I needed time to breathe.

"The church has one of the most wonderful families in the community, always donating their time and money to anything we need. Now they need our help. Now they are in a time of trouble. Someone has to be the link between that family and the church."

"And who is that?"

"Do you know Janette Turner? She is a dentist and cares for most of the kids in the community. Free of charge. She lives out in the suburbs, beautiful mansion, in a gated community out there, but she has returned to the city to care for her father. Her mother died three years ago. We did the funeral."

"What is her father sick with?" I was trying to fathom the cause of his concern.

"Dementia," the old man replied.

"Oh man, Terry's uncle had that. That's a horrible way to go."

"See, Janette wants to keep him out of the nursing home. She wants to keep him home with her, says she can take care of him. Says she lived a very self-centered life before now. She says it will prolong his life."

"What's her father's name?"

"Albert," the old man replied. "Janette says her father was responsible for her getting into dental school. He supported her all the way, despite her mother's objections. Janette never got along with her mother. They fought all of the time."

"Does she have any other family to share the burden?"

"Not really. She was an only child. There was a half brother, Ronnie, who enlisted in the Marines and has not been seen since."

"Is she married?"

"Once, to a fellow dentist. The marriage didn't take."

"Dr. Smart, what do you want me to do?"

There was a long pause on the line. Dr. Smart was thinking hard how to put the request into words. It was not a simple thing he was asking.

"Janette is going crazy with the pressures of her dental career and care giving for her father," the old man said. "She talked to me about putting her career on hold while she got him proper care. She worships her father. Probably you know that the Turner family was one of the main contributors to our building fund before he got sick."

"And?"

"And now these ghouls have surfaced from this faith healing church, the Witnesses of Christ Church, and they have weaseled into her life. These are the same crooks, excuse me, who were sentenced for their involvement in the death of a teenage girl. Two of their ring leaders were convicted of criminally negligent homicide. Now the church has sent members to camp out on her doorstep to influence her and her father's care."

I was puzzled. "What do they want, Dr. Smart?"

"See, the members of this faith healing circus don't like proper medical care," the old man explained. "They believe in all of this black magic, hoodoo, and smearing the sick with holy oil and the blood of goats. They also lay hands on the afflicted. It's that same mumbo-jumbo business."

"I don't understand. What do they want?"

"Money. They want her money. They don't give a care about her. Or her sick father. All they want is the money from the Turners."

"Why is this so important?" I asked. "Why don't we let Janette Turner sort this thing out by herself?"

"Because money doesn't grow on trees," the old man growled. "You must do this for me, for the church."

"What do you want from me?"

"I want you to charm her. You're my troubleshooter. You make problems go away. You're my spiritual envoy and I know what you can do."

"Dr. Smart, is her money that important?"

The question was a stupid one. All of the churches in the community were businesses, big businesses, with the chief commodity of selling and marketing the Lord and His Holy Word. Most of the preachers lived high on the hog, with fancy cars, fancy homes, spoiled wives and kids, and lots of women.

"Heck yes," the old man insisted. There was a gleam in his eyes. Greed.

"You still haven't said exactly what you want me to do."

A wicked chuckle sounded on the other end. "Charm the heck out of her. Do whatever is necessary to win her trust. Use your boyish good looks and confuse her. Turn her against them."

I was stunned. "I don't know if I can do what you ask."

"Not even for your church?"

"I don't know. You're asking a lot from me. I feel like a con man."

Dr. Smart was adamant. "You owe me. You owe us."

"What?" This was getting a bit weird.

"The church gave you back your life," the old man said. "You would be nothing without us, without our support and love."

"How can you ask me to do something like this?" I was beginning to see him for what he was and that was not a man of God. "I don't know if I can do this."

"Clint, you know you can do it and you will," the senior minister noted with certainty. "Everybody knows that you're sleeping with Claire Collier. And that's all right. A man needs to sow his wild oats sometimes. But you're not fooling anybody."

I was getting very upset. "That's none of your business."

"Oh yes, it is. Everything you do is my business." He talked to me like he was my handler, a puppeteer holding the strings.

"This is wrong," I said.

"No, it is not."

"We are no better than those snake handlers out there if we do this. We are taking advantage of her crisis. We are doing the same thing that these crooks want to do to her. It's not right. I don't care how we rationalize it."

"When did you become such a goody two-shoes?"

"I'm a Christian," I said. "I try to treat everybody like Jesus Christ would have treated them. I believe in the Bible."

"So do I . . . darn it!"

"How can you ask me to do this?"

"Because you can. It's easy for you. Women love you. You can make them do anything you want. I wish I had that magic. When I was a young man I had it, but when you get older you lose it somehow."

"I'm not Don Juan," I shouted. "Get yourself another boy."

Dr. Smart laughed crudely. "You'll do it or I'll ruin you. I'll smear your name all over the community, all over the city. Just as I made you, I can break your holier-than-thou butt."

I was rocked by my mentor's slimy intentions. "You can't do this."

"Oh yes, I can and I will."

The old man gave me Janette's phone number, ordered me to write it down, and told me to call her and get back to him with her response.

"Don't call me until you talk to her," Dr. Smart said. He swore at me a couple times, and hung up rudely.

After the call, I sat quietly on the sofa, staring at the telephone, not believing the conversation I had just experienced.

It was after two in the morning when I arrived to Claire's apartment. I was drenched from the rain, which was transforming the snow into a gray slush gathered at the curb. The woman, dressed in a terrycloth robe, pulled open the door and allowed me to shake off the water from my slicker.

I was still angry. I glared at her before sitting at the dining table. My stare washed over everything in the room. She noticed my outrage from the clenched fists, the lines around my mouth, and the jut of my jaw.

"Did you notice the time, Clint?" she asked, slightly annoyed.

My head lowered but the hands were busy in aggression. "I'm sorry."

"What's the problem, Reverend?"

I couldn't look at her. I was ashamed for how I surrendered my will to the elderly man who I thought was my mentor. "I was a fool . . . a simple fool . . . He conned me like a school kid."

"Dr. Smart . . . What did he do?" She knew exactly who I was talking about.

"I thought he was a friend. I thought he was supporting me through my loss, my grief, my sorrow, but he was only trying to get somebody to do his bidding.

He needed a puppet. He needed a robot to follow his orders."

She stood, watching me. "You did some wonderful things on behalf of the church and him. I don't see where you did something wrong."

My eyes went in her direction. "He knows about us."

"So, who cares?" she replied.

"Did you tell him about us?" I scanned her fully.

"No, but people talk," she said. "Do you think we are wrong?"

I sagged back in my chair. "I didn't say that."

She went to the kitchen, her voice trailing behind her, and got the pitcher of cold water from the refrigerator. She filled two glasses and bought them back to the table.

"Reverend, when I was married, I loved being in love," she said. "My husband was so romantic, so unpredictable. He loved surprising me. I loved the sexual heat, the spontaneity, just the theatre of it. He loved doing things in a big way. He took me on trips, bought me clothes, flowers, jewelry. He was all man. And I loved him very much."

I drank the water and tried to concentrate on my options. "Maybe I can talk to Dr. Smart; maybe he'll listen to reason."

"Why are you so angry?" she asked. "If you don't like something he did, why don't you go to the elders of the church?"

"I'm not angry." I frowned at her smug expression. I explained the scheme to get Janette Turner's money into the church's building fund with a few well-placed lies. I was the errand boy.

"Are you going to call this Janette woman?"

"No, I don't think so."

All I wanted to do was to go back to my life. I didn't like the trap Dr. Smart had created for me. *This stinking scheme.* I had this nagging headache since all of this started. It would not go away. As Claire saw it, I was just another guy with a share of stupid problems and a greedy mentor.

She drank her water and set the empty glass on the table. "Aren't you wasting your time? Dr. Smart isn't a fool. I understand it. He and his crowd want to live well. Everybody does. The elders of the church want to live well. And they know you can do it for them."

I refused to believe any of it. "Dr. Smart's not making sense. I cannot believe he's the same guy I trusted before. He has been lying to me all the time. He has been making a fool out of me."

She walked to the bathroom, splashed water on her face to wake up. A look in the mirror assured her that she was intact. When she returned, I was looking at a frayed copy of *Essence* proclaiming the renewal of the marriage vows. Beyonce was on the cover, showing off her curves. Claire's eyebrows lifted with cynicism as I leafed through the pages.

"Reverend, maybe Dr. Smart is jealous," she said icily. "Everybody knows that he steps out on his wife. He doesn't miss a trick. He doesn't like me because I slept with one of his deacons while I was going through a rough period in my marriage. His roguish reputation is popular knowledge."

"So that's why he doesn't like you," I replied.

"In fact, I was in a swank shoe store with his wife. She doesn't deserve him. She's a very elegant lady. We got to talking. She knows her husband well. She told some ladies I know that she was bored, lonely, upset, and pursued other men outside of their marriage. Some of them were his friends."

"Oh, man. . . ."

She took the glasses and lifted them. "Do you want something stronger?"

"No, but you got to fill me in on the old man."

She gave me a glass of water and some pills. I took them because my head was pounding like an angry drumbeat.

"Do you want to leave?" she asked, looking back at the door.

I sagged in pain. "I feel sick. I don't feel so good."

"What are you going to do about the Dr. Smart matter?"

"To heck with that," I shot back.

She gulped down her drink and laughed shamelessly, ignoring my discomfort. "You turn me on, Reverend. You know the effect you have on women. That's the truth."

"Claire, don't talk to me like that. I didn't come here for that. I just wanted to talk to you. I got a lot on my mind."

She pinched her nose. "Something sexy?"

"No, nothing like that."

"Well, we can talk. You have no idea how much fun you were. You're a real tease."

"Nothing happened, just a little kissing and hugging." I was trying to remain focused on the matter at hand. I felt exhausted.

"Anticipation is the best part of it." She laughed.

I rose and backed away from her. My intention was to get as far away from her as possible. She started to undress me. Her slender hands were lifting my shirt in back as she corralled me against the wall. My brain said no, heck no; this was not why I came here. I needed a friend, not a lover now.

"Could you stop that, please?" I squirmed.

She was staring at me, her eyes very intense. In my mental fog, I could see her mouthing the words, something about going to the toilet and freshening up. I noticed that all the lights were off, with the only glow provided by the moonlight through the half-open blinds.

I shook my head. *No, not this time.*

Then I saw the whole room spinning, the furniture spinning, the walls spinning, the woman spinning. I needed to sit down before I fell down. I went over in a mess of arms and legs, holding my face in my hands, and then slid down to the pinewood floor.

When I awoke later, I was naked under the slightly soiled sheets in her big brass bed. I pulled myself out from the covers and stood there, watching quietly the sleeping beauty at rest.

Claire lay on her stomach, her pretty head almost obscured by one of the silk pillows. A shapely leg was tossed over the other. I could see her nakedness exposed and perspiring as well as her wolfish grin on her sweating, seductive face.

I gathered my pants, shirt, and briefs in one hand and started for the bathroom. She said something in her sleep, muffled, but I couldn't make it out. I couldn't remember anything about that previous night. And maybe that was best.

CHAPTER 25

CUT TO THE QUICK

Wherefore, if God so clothe the grass of the field, which today is, and tomorrow is cast into the oven, shall he not much more clothe you. O ye of little faith?

—Matthew 6:30

On a night exactly like this, I had problems sleeping. My doctor prescribed strong sleeping medication, something that could give me a decent night's rest, but worry and stress always kept me up until all hours. I never could get the proper amount of rest. That was why I'd collapsed the other night.

I found myself sitting up in the bed one night, trembling from a case of nerves. Nightmares were common for me. It seemed there was no peace for me since the tragedy happened.

The curtains were flapping as if they were being blown by a mysterious wind; the clothes and shoes were floating in air at waist level. There was a sinister pale brilliance in the room and then I saw it. It was Terry, a young Terry, in her cream wedding dress, just as she was at the start of our journey together.

It was unthinkable. Her ashen face was bruised and swollen, with a gaping hole in her neck. I found myself unable to breathe. I couldn't cry out. But I couldn't look away from the hideous sight. I gagged. My skin crawled with goose bumps while I saw her spinning above the room, spinning above the furniture, the crimson droplets splashing along the length of the walls. Everything was in slow motion. Blood flowed in a string of red pearls from her torn neck, to the long, stylish dress, to her bare brown legs and feet.

I watched in trembling terror, with my hand clamped over my mouth. Can you sacrifice one thing to get another?

I held my nose at the odor. The stench in the room was a mix of decaying flesh, the odor of drying blood, and a flowery perfume. My heart vibrated in the center of my chest.

The harsh moment of discovery. I relived it all over again, the horrible second I discovered her body, the pooled blood, unmoving, grotesquely still. I knelt beside her and felt for a pulse. There was no stirring in her silent bosom. No heartbeat. Although I could see where the bullet went into her body, I hoped that when I put my ear against her open mouth that I would sense life. Oh sweet Jesus, oh sweet Jesus.

"Envy." My wife's voice was a sultry whisper.

I was so startled at its sound. I couldn't believe it.

Her body spun in a tight, rhythmic circle. "You never loved me or these children," she said softly and feminine, completely normal. "You loved other things more than us."

Finally, she turned to face me, a malicious smile on her ruined face. "Satan wants you bad, very bad." She gave out a low whistle. "Why won't you give him what he wants?" I heard something between the sounds of the words: a muffled cry, a dark moan.

At that point, I wanted to be rid of these feelings of guilt and desperation, for once and for all. I

*didn't care about the existence of evil or an afterlife.
I wanted Terry, my beautiful wife and the mother of
my children, back with me. I wanted them back in my
life.*

"Envy," she repeated shrilly.

"Be gone, Satan!" I blurted out.

How can you have hope for the future?

I lay with a long golden cross of the crucified Christ
in my clasped hands, trying to blot out all clutter from
my mind. I wanted to pray, needed to pray. I couldn't
stop crying. The tears rolled down my cheeks so I took
a handkerchief from the dresser and wiped my face
roughly. *Stop feeling sorry for yourself.* I caught my
wind, stopped sobbing, and sat up, dangling my legs off
the bed. Suddenly, a blissful smile covered my face and
I knew I was going to be all right.

This nightmarish vision was incredibly scary but it
provided me with a comfort that I never knew existed
before. A tremendous calm suddenly came over me.
Somehow I felt protected by the vision. The odd thing
was there was no fear or doubt in me now. I didn't
know why.

Still, I know I was not alone. I felt the power of the
Lord in me. My back went limp and I slid sideways under the covers. Soon I was sound asleep.

CHAPTER 26

THE PURE IN HEART

But I have prayed for thee, that thy faith fail not; and when thou art converted, strengthen thy brethren.

—Luke 22:32

When I arrived to my aunt's place, the attendant showed me right inside her room. She was watching the golden glow of an astounding sunset, her hands folded across her chest holding a frayed pamphlet about the resurrection of the Lord. I stood in the doorway, looking at her watching the wonder of the creation.

"You're in a world of trouble, mister," my aunt said, without turning around. "Good and evil cannot be destroyed. It will always be here."

I pulled up a chair. "So you've heard the gossip?"

My aunt looked out of one window, then the other. "People aren't themselves in these difficult days, including Christians. They're worse than the sinners."

"The rumor in the church is that I'm having sex with Miss Collier," I said. "I'll admit that I went over to her apartment but nothing happened. Somebody wants to drag me through the mud."

Thinking back to that crazy night, although I woke up naked in her apartment, we didn't have sex. I wanted to touch her badly because it had been a long time since Terry. But I knew all about lust since I had suffered through Terry's lust. I didn't want that in my life.

"You've always had a target on your back," she said.

"Why would somebody do something like this?"

She coughed and cleared her throat. "This is the work of the devil. This is a cruel game. Dr. Smart, the man, is not a good shepherd. He's a terrible liar. I think you know that."

"Yes," I replied.

"Christians should not evade the truth," she continued. "Tell me, poor boy, what does he want you to do this time?"

Dr. Smart was worse than that. He was what my father used to call a jackleg. A shyster. I told her what the old minister requested of me, courting the widow to get a hold of the funds needed to line their pockets. I wondered why he would ask something so against my morals and values, unless he thought he could control me.

"Don't let him lead you down a wrong path," my aunt said, now pivoting toward me with a look of distaste on her aged face.

"I've always done what he asked me to do," I confessed. "I did everything he wanted. But this thing isn't right."

"And that's why he thought he could make a fool out of you," she said, wheeling herself opposite to my seat so I could see every expression on her face.

"But he is wrong about this," I assured her. "I've come too far to be backsliding. God created the world good. Christians should be doing good, not doing some dirt like this scheme."

My aunt glanced out of the corner of her eye. "The whole sky is orange. Did you notice that?"

"Yes, I did."

"Dr. Smart and his cronies are leeches," she said. "God wants us to praise Him. God wants us to be one, of one mind, to worship Him. He has set up the church to do just that. We must love and respect one another. If man keeps turning away from God, then man will pay for his disobedience."

"I feel like I'm Dr. Smart's accomplice," I joked.

"You are," she said. "But you can't do this thing."

"I know," I said sadly. "I can't figure him out. It's almost like he wants me to fail. He wants me to sin and go to hell."

"That's why your faith is so important," she said.

"Sometimes I can feel Dr. Smart and the elders thinking I will never be normal, never be whole again. One of them told me that 'I must put off my old self and clean up my spiritual environment.' Sometimes I could feel them gloating at my suffering and my misfortune. They thought the Lord had taken me down a peg. That's not what Christians should be about. This has been a rude awakening. Also, it's always strange to see yourself as others see you."

"This life is a short one," my aunt said. "You know I always say that."

"I know you do, auntie."

"We came into this life with nothing and we'll leave this life with nothing."

I had heard this all before. Old people, when they get a certain age, focus on death and the passage of time. "I know we are all going to die. I know that. We all know that. But what has that to do with what Dr. Smart and the elders want me to do?"

She laughed quietly, holding out her withered hand. "Faith shows us that we should take personal responsibility for our actions. God refreshes faith. He wants us to make wise, responsible choices."

I took her hand, smiling at her wisdom. "He is in us, all of us."

She kept some biblical truths to herself, but her faith as a rock-steady Christian was sound and solid. Her finger pointed at her heart as she leaned forward and said in a firm voice, "Clint, you must put God first. You cannot act apart from the will of God. You must obey Him. Everything you think you know and believe about God will be tested. And not just by sinners, as you well know."

I needed this pep talk. I nodded to the soulful cadence of her voice while she went on about the power of the Lord.

"God is in control." She grinned. "All you need to do is ask Him to take you where He wants you to go. That's that. You must know that God will be God no matter what happens."

A knock on the door interrupted us. A young Latina said that there would be a piano recital in the recreation room. My aunt didn't growl at her but she put on a mask of annoyance. She ignored her and the woman left.

"We're lost sheep," I mumbled. "How do I know I'm right?"

"Because you are right, that's all."

"If the church falls into the traps of greed, deception, and sin, then we as Christians are finished," I moaned. "Some people say God isn't speaking anymore. Some people say God is dead."

"God has His own timetable," she said. "He doesn't move by man's schedule. Don't surrender to the easy way. Don't give in to sin."

"What do I do if Dr. Smart makes good on his blackmail threat?"

My aunt moved closer still toward me. I looked at her with soft, pleading eyes. With the pride of a strong black woman who had seen so much in her day, she squeezed my hand tightly and stared at my expression as if she could see into my soul.

"If you live long enough, you discover that wisdom is a continuing process," she said. "You must change the way you look at things. God is God and He will never allow anything to come into your life that He wouldn't use for your own good."

"I thought about that on the way over to see you," I answered. "I know the Lord is not punishing me. I don't see myself as a victim."

"Be honest with me." My aunt cocked her head and asked me, "Did you do any hanky-panky with her?"

"No, ma'am."

"Now you mad at me for asking that question, right?"

"No, I'm not. Miss Collier knows her way around the block. She probably worked it out with him so he would think I made love to her. I didn't play her. She played me. She hugged and kissed me and messed up my mind. She dogged me. She used me."

"See, you're wrong there," she replied. "She didn't get anything."

"I know she didn't," I admitted.

"Do you know what we used to call women like Miss Collier?"

I shook my head. I didn't know.

"They called women like Miss Collier a trollop and worse," she replied. "She's not the woman for you. A little loose. Also, these folks sitting on the church pews haven't got any feelings at all. If these church people really knew what Dr. Smart and the elders were up to, they would run him out of town on a rail."

We laughed at that one until our eyes filled with tears.

Thinking of Terry, I wondered if that term, trollop, could be applied to her as well. "I want someone who isn't plotting and planning. A schemer. I want a woman who lets me wear the pants sometimes. I had one of those gals who thought she could think for both of us."

Nothing I said during my visit surprised my aunt. We steered the talk away from the clever Miss Collier, the devious Dr. Smart, and talked about baseball and the rivalry between the Yankees and the Red Sox. Suddenly, she asked me to lock the door, and wheeled herself into the center of the room.

"Hand me that cane behind the closet door." She chuckled snidely and stepped on the tiled floor. "Time to get some exercise, my dear."

"Why do you need the wheelchair?"

"Everybody wants to get special attention around here." She laughed. "That's what this place is for. Let folks wait on you."

I smiled. "I see."

As she walked in tight, little circles around the room, she kept up a brisk pace until she worked up a little sweat. "Now, you know what I would like? Something that would be good right about now?"

"No, I don't."

"A cold glass of red Kool-Aid, real tall and frosty." She giggled like a schoolgirl and kept on stepping.

CHAPTER 27

YOU'RE NOT THAT KIND

Above all, taking the shield of faith, wherewith ye shall be able to quench all the fiery darts of the wicked.

—Ephesians 6:16

Sometimes I went to the local barber shop for a haircut, just to get my mind clear and listen to some adult chatter. While I waited for my turn in the chair, I sat and watched the small group of customers, hearing snatches of the conversations going on between the barbers and the men. I noticed the usual blue jokes, involving women and sex, were curtailed when I was there. They respected my position as a man of God, but that didn't mean that these black men didn't enjoy being among themselves in true fellowship.

"Reverend, how are you feeling these days?" one of the barbers asked, snipping with a pair of scissors some unruly kinks from a customer's head. "You haven't been in the shop for some time. We missed you."

A few of the men agreed with him, nodding in agreement, and even one or two patted me on the back. They knew of my loss and respected that.

"Keith, I've been busy with the Lord's work," I replied. "There's always somebody who needs the church at any moment of the day. Still, I know I need to get my hair cut. I looked in the mirror yesterday and I looked like a bush baby."

A customer with a close cut laughed out loud. "That's a good one."

"Did you hear on the news yesterday about the cops fixing tickets for their friends and relatives?" another barber asked no one in particular. "The papers said the police quashed the tickets after they were issued. That's against the law. Some of the cops were ratted out by other cops, who were taking bribes and favors from drug dealers in Harlem and the Bronx."

"I know one cop said the district attorney got his tickets fixed," a customer chimed in, with his face lathered up. "The mayor said the city has no tolerance for this kind of thing but he needs to see all of the evidence of the allegation. It'll be swept under the rug. No doubt."

I sat there, partially listening to the men, but the dilemma of serving as Dr. Smart's crony in scamming the woman was never far from my mind.

The barber, standing next to Keith, was reading from the newspaper. "After the cops' arraignments, the president of the Patrolmen's Benevolent Association, the union represents the police, said, 'Taking care of your family, taking care of your friends, is not a crime. To take a courtesy and turn it into a crime is wrong.'"

Another customer, with a bald pate, smirked. "A crook is a crook is a crook."

I thought about Dr. Smart, my mentor and master crook. *A Judas.*

"I know the cops who shot Sean Bell, the guy who was supposed to get married that next day, regret the day they ever fired fifty shots at him," said Amir, the dreadlocked barber. "He left a bachelor party and then the quick-shooting police riddle his car and him. They should fire them all."

"Meanwhile, these black boys see that and wonder why the police harass them," Keith added. "They're going about their business, just walking on the street or driving, and then they get stopped and frisked. Once they get into the system, they get criminalized. I think the cops have a quota. Do you, Reverend?"

"I think it's fishy," I answered. "I know random police stops don't save lives. They're a major part of the problem."

There was one barber, Joshua, whose chair I never sat in, because of his right-wing politics. Often the other barbers snickered at him when he messed up a head or let a customer linger in the chair to get a big tip.

"I felt sorry for the wife of Bernie Madoff when she said she loved her man and couldn't believe what he did to his friends," Joshua said. "She has no one. She has lost everything. She even lost her son. I really felt sad when she talked about how she missed her son, Mark, who hung himself with a dog leash. His baby was in the next room. I almost cried."

The customers rolled their eyes and moaned. Even the barbers mumbled at his phony show of compassion and sorrow. I laughed under my breath.

"Madoff robbed widows, orphans, even his best friends," Amir blasted. "He ran a sixty-five billion dollar scam without any regard for anybody. I think his wife, Ruth, knew what he was doing. He was a big-time scam artist."

"You don't know what you're talking about," Joshua replied. "I guess you'd like him better if he was some thug robbing a liquor store of forty dollars. White folk rob on a grander scale. That's just stupid."

Keith looked around the room, winked at me, and read from the newspaper taken from the barber next to him. "I don't know whose idea it was, but we decided to kill ourselves because it was so horrendous what was happening," he mimicked in a weak white woman's voice, the voice of Madoff's prison widow. "We had terrible phone calls. Hate mail, just beyond anything. We took pills. We couldn't live with ourselves anymore. We woke up the next day and I'm glad we woke up."

Everyone was howling with laughter. His impression of Bernie's wife was spot-on and cracked everybody up.

Baldie intoned, "A crook is a crook is a crook."

"What about Lindsay Lohan and her foolishness?" Amir asked.

Keith waved him off. "We don't mention her name in here."

"What about Miss Apple Bottom Booty and her quick marriage?" Joshua volunteered.

Keith intervened again. "None of that Kim K. stuff in here either."

I stood up, watching another patron with a messed-up haircut hoping to take my seat. The barbers would charge him a repair fee to make him look life-like. I started walking out, with Dr. Smart's blistering words ringing in my head.

"Going, Reverend?" Keith asked me.

"I just remembered that I've got something to do," I answered. A call to Reverend Hickory Peck, a friend I met at the West Coast seminar, was in order. Maybe he'd set me straight and advise me what course to take in the Smart matter. When we said our good-byes, he promised me that he would always find time to take my call.

Before the day ended, I called the church office of Reverend Peck, the minister of Strong Oak Community Church in Dixon, Alabama. His secretary replied the reverend was making his rounds at a food bank, putting in an appearance at a drop-in ministry for the homeless, and delivering three computers at a transitional shelter for battered women. I admired the hands-on approach of this Southern pastor who gave his time and energy back to his neighborhood.

"Reverend Peck works very hard spreading the Word of God," his secretary said. "He always says to us that we must be committed beyond praise. I'll tell him you called, sir. He'll call you back. Count on that."

I thanked her and hung up the phone. I walked around the apartment, wanting a smoke. The cigarette pack was on the coffee table in the living room.

I stared at it, picked it up, and tossed it in the garbage.

With my mind still buzzing, I fell asleep on the couch and didn't awake until the phone was ringing for some time. I thought it would be the church but it was Reverend Peck calling from some sleepy Alabama road. There was some static on the other end.

A husky voice I immediately recognized as Reverend Hickory Peck appeared through the hiss. "Hello, my brother, I just got your message. I've pulled over. It's raining cats and dogs here. They say we might get a hurricane. I hope not. We don't need that much water."

I was honored that the reverend would talk to me. "Thanks for returning my call. You said if I needed some advice, I could give you a call."

He laughed. "That's what I said. Now, how can I help you?"

"You know I explained how Dr. Smart served as my mentor," I said. "In fact, he was responsible for my attendance to the seminar. Dr. Smart did me a great service but now he's asking me to do something that goes against my faith."

"What is he asking you to do?" Reverend Peck was very direct.

"I don't know where to start," I stammered. "Dr. Smart is asking me to act as a gigolo to a rich woman to con her into giving money to the church. I don't think that's right."

I could hear the windshield wipers struggling against the driving rain. What I couldn't hear was the pastor thinking of a practical solution to my crisis before answering. He was a very thoughtful man.

The reverend coughed slightly before replying. "Remember one of our talks under the trees out there? Like yourself, I told you then, I never feel abandoned by God. Do you know why that is? Because I can always feel His hand in my life, always."

"What does that have to do with Dr. Smart and this church scam?"

The reverend laughed again. "Hold your horses . . ."

It was like waiting for a climax at the end of a mystery movie, where all of the accounts were settled and the bad guy was caught.

"I feel for you, brother," he said. "I hate that Dr. Smart betrayed you, because you admired and respected him so much. Let me say this. Some people will want you to fail; some people will want you to fall down on the job. But you must lead by example. We are the living embodiment of His Holy Word. You must not ask people to do anything that you wouldn't do yourself."

"What?" I didn't know where he was going with this.

"Show the congregation you care," the reverend said. "Let them see you choose the right thing. Don't mislead them."

"Uh-huh." I agreed with him.

The reverend, known for his rural wisdom, showed me why he was such a great teacher. He was not only a good listener, but an excellent reader of the human spirit. We had talked during the seminar about the founding of a credit union where hard-working people could save and borrow money for things that would sustain them. He also discussed buying large parcels of land to build affordable housing, for there was still a great deal of racism in the lending practices among the banks.

"What Dr. Smart feels is that he can embrace the things of the world and still follow God," he continued. "Your mentor hoped he could lure you into the web of corruption with him. He didn't realize that you had grown emotionally and spiritually, that you had been renewed by the fire of your tragedies."

"That's true," I said. I'd learned a lot in the last few months.

"That's what I try to practice each and every day," the reverend said. "I try to obey God and live holy. I humble myself and live right."

"I try to do that as well."

"As messengers of our faith, I take time and listen to my flock. What do you think of the good Dr. Smart as a man and as a Christian?"

"I think he's a flawed man," I admitted. "Before my eyes were opened by this, I thought he sat on the right hand of the Lord. I idolized him."

"Dr. Smart's a man, human," the reverend said. "Never forget that."

"I know. . . ."

"As I said, Dr. Smart wants it both ways and no Christian can do that," he acknowledged. "You can't serve two masters. Every time someone tries to do that, they're bound to fail."

"Yes, sir." He was right about my old mentor.

"Dr. Smart is a sinner and that's that. The problem with Dr. Smart and our community is that they feel that they can confess their sins and sin again. Our race will not let God work in our hearts. You see, our elders opened their hearts to God and that alone gave them the strength to survive slavery and Jim Crow."

"Amen to that." I smiled and nodded.

"Brother Clint, you must evaluate the quality of your faith," the reverend went on. "Ask yourself what it means to be a Christian, what it means to follow the Lord. Then ask yourself how those things measure up against Dr. Smart's wicked request."

I listened to what Reverend Peck said and weighed my options.

"Look at your spiritual gifts," he said. "See with the eyes of the Holy Spirit. Hear the voice of God through your prayers and meditation. Truly listen to the Lord."

"Should I do this thing that Dr. Smart asks?"

"You know the answer to that," he said. "You've come through life's trials better and not bitter. Don't seek to please people. Live to please God."

"So you're saying I should pray to get my answers?"

"Praying is good," the reverend replied. "We can always get answers to our prayers. But sometimes it's just not going to happen like we want it to happen."

"Do I do what Dr. Smart asks?" I repeated.

"Only you know the answer to that. Follow God's Word."

I was frustrated. "I'm tired of people using the church for self-serving purposes. Maybe I should walk away from the church and Dr. Smart."

"You don't mean that," the reverend said calmly. "If you do walk away, you can always come down and join our church. We'd be glad to have you. We need some young blood. We always need to reenergize this place. We'd welcome you."

"Thanks, Reverend Peck."

"Now, I've got to go," the reverend concluded. "Give me a call and let me know what you decide. God bless."

And then he was gone.

CHAPTER 28

IN FULL STRIDE

A faithful man shall abound with blessings;
but he that maketh haste to be rich shall not be
innocent.

—Proverbs 27:6

In the days after the crazed talk with Dr. Smart, I couldn't eat, couldn't sleep, couldn't speak to anybody. I especially avoided any contact with the old man, his group of elders, or anyone affiliated with the leadership of the church. The following day after our confrontation, I tried to call him but he wouldn't come to the phone. I dialed his private line.

No luck. He was freezing me out until I accomplished what he wanted me to do. Any form of communication was dead until I did as I was told. Text, e-mail, or phone. Nothing.

The real issue was that Dr. Smart had lied. He betrayed me, betrayed the church, betrayed the Lord. I knew the world lied about everything and anything. All I required from him was the truth. The old man wisely told me that truth is flexible and can be easily manipulated.

"I could have told you that Dr. Smart is a liar," Claire said to me. "There is no such thing to him as a half lie or a white lie. You can't believe anything he says. If his mouth is moving, he's lying and all he wants is to better himself. God has nothing to do with it."

"I know that," I replied. "But I didn't think the old man would lie to me. I trusted him. I trusted him like a father."

"Don't let him force you to do something you will hate."

Dr. Smart was nothing better than a jackleg preacher and a clever swindler. He didn't know the meaning of truth. Also, I recalled the talk with Reverend Peck and the promise of a renewed Christian life.

"Clint, don't let him suck you in," Claire said. "He's dangerous."

"He wants to take credit for the restoration of my faith," I said sourly. "But you know that dealing with life has taught me to care and nourish my soul. Not him. From the lessons of the last few months, I have learned that faith is essential to human resilience, happiness, and serenity. Not him."

Claire laughed. "Now you're figuring it out. God opened doors for you and Dr. Smart. Only He can steer you to the truth."

I spent the better part of two years trying to solve the riddle of my wife, with her mental confusion and sexual mayhem. After the death of Terry and the kids, I wandered through life, trying to keep my mind off the tragedy and grief. I had never felt such despair. It gnawed away at my spirit. It shouted gibberish in my mind. It wouldn't let me rest with its tortured pictures of the last moments of my children on earth.

"Does being with me help?" she asked.

"You know it does." I didn't mind the fact that she wanted to hear me say how important she was to my recovery. It was true.

For some reason, I was waiting to be intimate with her. The kisses and embraces sufficed for now, but I was finding it hard to be so restrained. I fought down any notions of hot desire. That was why when Dr. Smart threatened me with letting the cat out of the bag, I laughed because he didn't know I still treated Claire Collier like a lady.

We both respected each other's boundaries. Senseless death had wrapped itself around us very tightly. She realized I needed much healing internally. Even my soul was in need of repair.

In those dark, desperate months after their needless deaths, I functioned and managed to appear normal. I wanted my family back. I wanted my wife, Terry, back. God strengthened me beyond madness and idleness. One thing I discovered was everybody went through something like this at least once in their lives.

"Just imagine that Dr. Smart is dead and that you have just lost another loved one," she suggested. "You will get over this. You will survive. But you cannot let this get you down."

"He fooled me," I confessed. "He really did."

"No, Dr. Smart knew you were ambitious and he kept building you up," she said. "He knew what he was doing."

I was in over my head. I took my eye off the ball. He realized that I was getting ambitious and steered my energy in that direction. I needed a harsh slap to the head.

"Do what you think is right," she insisted.

This moment was crucial. I could see this trap so clearly. It never entered my mind to confront him, to battle him for the high ground, and to strip away his hypocrisy. He was betting on my low-key persona. If I felt terrified or passive, the old man and his cronies would walk all over me.

"Does this make you leery about the church?" she asked.

"I am a Christian and will always be," I said proudly. "This foolishness has nothing to do with the teachings of Christ."

And I meant that. The church was not my enemy. God was my strength. For once, I realized that I couldn't control my life or the world. *If I am going to heal my tattered soul, if I am going to recover, I must feel whole in my faith.* I had to embrace God fully.

"What are you going to say to Dr. Smart the next time you talk to him?" she asked, satisfied that I would stick to my guns.

"I'll give him an earful," I said.

The church has nothing to do with a few rotten apples who try to pervert its cause. Money will not get you into heaven. Greed will not get a seat next to the Master.

There was a verse I'd come across in the Bible, something very appropriate from Proverbs 19:21. It read:

Many are the plans in a man's heart, but it is the Lord's purpose that prevails.

I refused to be scandalized by the corruption of Dr. Smart and his select few of the elders who let their greed overcome them.

Claire asked me to come by after my evening walk. It was my custom to walk from my home through the park to the mall. My legs needed the exercise, while it gave me time to allow my mind to quiet itself.

As I walked through the park, I paused to look up at the orange moon. There was a sizeable amount of wind, forceful but less than a gale. The streets were icy and frozen since the temperature had dropped. Houses along the park and the side streets were quiet, lit, with shadows appearing from time to time in their windows.

What my aunt kept saying was that I deserved the good things in life. I should never give up and settle for less. For so long, I felt I deserved what I got. Finally she showed me, with God's help, that I was not undeserving.

My cell phone rang. I answered and continued walking toward Claire's house. "Hello? Who is it?"

A familiar, deep-throated voice replied, "Hey, It's Deacon Little. You asked me to check on some things for you. You wanted to know what Dr. Smart really needed the money for, right?"

"That's right." I stopped mid-step and listened.

"He needs the cash for his son," the deacon said.

"What son?"

"Dr. Smart has an outside son, a love child by this exotic dancer," the deacon revealed. "He was hooked up with her a long time ago. The son is about twenty-five years old. It seems his son got mixed up with this nurse and they were talking about getting married. She wanted him to move back to Louisiana with her."

"But what happened?"

"Well, there was a child involved with the woman," the deacon said. "The child was this other guy's son. The child must be around seven. She had jilted this guy to be with Dr. Smart's son so anyway, this guy catches up to his ex in a parking lot and starts to jerk her around. Dr. Smart's son runs to her rescue and tackles the guy, but he pulls a gun and fires two bullets into our hero's chest."

"I guess the son's almost dead?" I didn't want to ask.

"Very nearly. He's on life support out in a hospital in the Bronx. Dr. Smart keeps him alive and he needs some money. Desperately. That's why he put so much pressure on you to deliver the money."

"Oh man. . . ."

"There's more," Deacon Little added. "One of the other deacons, Deacon Cannon, discovered there was a considerable sum of money missing from the church treasury. He confronted Dr. Smart yesterday with the theft. At first, the old man denied knowing anything about it but the good deacon and his group broke him down."

I was stunned, absolutely shocked. "Where is Dr. Smart now?" I asked.

"In jail," Deacon Little said drily.

Now I started crossing the street when this car began weaving in a crazy manner, running two red lights, suddenly lurching into a speed meant for highway traffic. Strangely, I had the eerie impression that somebody, a presence, was standing beside me and ready to shove me if I didn't move right away. In that instant, I leaped on a parked car, on its hood, while the speeding vehicle scraped past in a blur, showering me with a giant spray of sparks.

The hand of God touched me at that second. It was a divine warning. To this day, I can't explain why I felt that force, that glowing energy, when there was no one there, and I leaped out of the way of certain death. I guess it was not my time.

The car plowed through people, sending bodies flying into the air, sometimes smashing into the parked autos, and moving on. People were crying and screaming.

Even when I ran toward the crowd gathered around the injured and dead, I sensed a presence running alongside with me.

The crowd rushed to help the injured. I saw one of the people wounded by the racing car, going sailing over its hood with an echoing bang, flying in the air to crash solidly against the pavement.

"Oh my God," screamed a mother, shielding the eyes of her children while she hustled them away.

There were several pedestrians mowed down by the car and many of them were sprawled in the street, some seriously injured. A group of the onlookers had chased the car and dragged the driver out, punching and kicking him as he fell down. The car had a shattered windshield and several dents in its hood.

The battered driver kept saying, "The gas pedal stuck . . . Tried to stop . . . and it started speeding up . . . Forgive me . . . Forgive me . . . Didn't want to hurt anybody." They continued to beat and kick him viciously until he passed out.

I ran over to one of the fallen. I turned up my collar and knelt down to the seriously injured man. His eyes were glassy. Blood covered his face and hands, and was soaking through his clothes. A dog was licking the red liquid near his head on the pavement when someone chased it away.

The man was struggling to say something but nothing came out. The onlookers remained glued to the spot, wanting to see the ultimate event. The death of another soul. The end of life. *Ghouls.* Someone let out a sob.

A woman, dressed fashionably, got on her knees as the man's body shook and she stroked his hair and the back of his neck. The dying man looked at me curiously. It was almost as if the man was trying to get something straight in his head. He seemed to be in shock.

The man was panting, trying to catch his ragged breath. He was near the end of his life. The crowd pressed in on him, looking, attempting to see everything, even his last breath. There was no fear in his eyes. He was prepared for his death. There were the sounds of ambulance sirens racing to the scene, drawing near, but they would be too late.

"I . . . I . . . will be fine," the man rasped. I knelt closer, as did the woman who held his bloody hand. "Trust in . . . in . . . God . . . not in man."

That gave me gooseflesh. He died before the ambulances arrived. I said a prayer and walked away from the carnage.

I feel God saved me. He saved me in more ways than one. It was as if He was saying: I want you to know that I am God and I will always be with you.

I kept repeating what the dying man had said with his last breath. "Trust in God, not in man." It didn't matter that Dr. Smart was behind bars. A final lesson had been learned in this terrible ordeal. What did matter was that anyone can be tricked or swayed by the charm of a false prophet, but the importance of a saved life rested in the transformative power of God. There were many ministers who supposedly specialized in saving souls, steering the flock away from hurt and harm, but nobody and nothing could top the salvation that came from the Lord. That was the answer. That was the divine truth.

UC HIS GLORY BOOK CLUB!
www.uchisglorybookclub.net

UC His Glory Book Club is the spirit-inspired brainchild of Joylynn Jossel, Author and Acquisitions Editor of Urban Christian, and Kendra Norman-Bellamy, Author for Urban Christian. This is an online book club that hosts authors of Urban Christian. We welcome as members all men and women who have a passion for reading Christian-based fiction.

UC HIS GLORY BOOK CLUB pledges our commitment to provide support, positive feedback, encouragement, and a forum whereby members can openly discuss and review the literary works of Urban Christian authors.

There is no membership fee associated with UC His Glory Book Club; however, we do ask that you support the authors through purchasing, encouraging, providing book reviews, and of course, your prayers. We also ask that you respect our beliefs and follow the guidelines of the book club. We hope to receive your valuable input, opinions, and reviews that build up, rather than tear down our authors.

WHAT WE BELIEVE:

—We believe that Jesus is the Christ, Son of the Living God
—We believe the Bible is the true, living Word of God
—We believe all Urban Christian authors should use their God-given writing abilities to honor God and share the message of the written word God has given to each of them uniquely.
—We believe in supporting Urban Christian authors in their literary endeavors by reading, purchasing and sharing their titles with our online community.
—We believe that in everything we do in our literary arena should be done in a manner that will lead to God being glorified and honored.

We look forward to the online fellowship with you. Please visit us often at *www.uchisglorybookclub.net.*

Many Blessing to You!
Shelia E. Lipsey,
President, UC His Glory Book Club

Notes